Magic & Monsters

LARCHWOOD CORRECTIVE ACADEMY 2

USA TODAY BESTSELLING AUTHOR

C.J. PINARD

This book is an original publication of Pinard House Publishing.

This is a work of fiction. The names, characters, places, and incidents are products of the writer's imagination or have been used fictitiously and are not to be construed as real. Any resemblance to persons, living or dead, actual events, locales, or organizations is entirely coincidental.

Copyright © 2021-2022 Pinard House Publishing, LLC

This is licensed for your personal enjoyment only. No part of this book may be reproduced, scanned, or distributed in any printed or electronic format without permission. Please do not participate in, or encourage, piracy of copyrighted materials in violation of the author's rights. Purchase only authorized editions.

All rights reserved.

PRINTED IN THE UNITED STATES OF AMERICA

ISBN: 9798718920437

Acknowledgements

Cover Art by Kellie Dennis at Book Cover by Design
Copyediting by Amabel Daniels
Editing and Title by Emma Shade

LARCHWOOD CORRECTIVE ACADEMY SERIES

Curses & Charm

Monsters & Magic

Runes & Rituals

Secrets & Spells

Chapter 1

More anxious than I care to admit, I sit in Magic 101 on the first day of class and wait for the headmaster to come strolling in. I can't help but glance at the door more often than is considered appropriate, and of course, these actions don't go unnoticed by my witch bestie Astrid, who's seated behind me.

"He's gonna be here soon, just chill," she says, putting her hand on my shoulder.

"I have no idea what you're talking about." I sniff, avoiding turning around to look at her.

She laughs. "Your aura is a very horny green."

Now, I turn around and stare into my best friend's eyes, the same color as my alleged aura. "There's no such thing as auras."

Astrid winks. "That's what you think. Just started seeing them recently."

"No way," I say, eyes wide. "You've got to be shi—"

"Hello, class. Please take your seats."

I whip around when I see Headmaster Anton Griggs walk into the room. Looking fine as hell in a black button-down shirt, shiny sky-blue tie, and black dress slacks.

"You're welcome." Astrid chuckles behind me.

I should thank her for distracting me from the sexy headmaster as he swaggers into the room.

"Most of you know me as Mr. Griggs, and I'm tasked with teaching all you fine witches and warlocks Magic 101."

He writes his name and the course name on the whiteboard

behind him.

"As for the course's title—for the record, I'm not the one who chose it. It was established long before I came to Larchwood."

"I think it's a very appropriate title," Astrid interjects.

Brown-noser.

"Well, thank you, Ms. Marx."

She beams at him.

He briefly glances at me before putting his eyes back on the crowd of students. There's about 30 of us in this class, so no way is he gonna get away with ogling me. That doesn't mean I can't ogle him, though.

"We'll start with an icebreaker," he begins. "Raise your hand if you knew all your life that you were a witch or warlock."

Nearly the entire class raises their hand. Just me, a guy in the back, and one of the girls who had been in the county clink with me before we came here. I think her name is Alicia.

He looks at her. "Miss Vazquez, how come you didn't know you were a witch?"

"I spent my life in the foster care system," she says quietly while sliding some black hair behind her ear.

The room is deathly quiet.

Poor Alicia. That blows.

"That's unfortunate," he replies. "Care to tell us your story?"

She shakes her head and looks down.

"Understandable. Well, everything you didn't learn from family, you're going to learn here. So chin up, young lady."

I stifle a laugh at his term of endearment. He talks like a grandpa. What is he, eight years older than us? Ten, maybe?

She nods and smiles at him.

"What about you, Miss Masset?" Griggs turns his attention to me, staring at me with those intense baby blues. "Thought you were raised by witches."

"I was," I reply. "My mom didn't bother telling me I was a witch until I became a teen."

He nods. "Well, why not, if you don't mind me asking?"

His formality is sort of annoying me, but I tamp down on my irritation and tell myself he has to behave like a teacher, not a hot warlock for whom I want to get on my knees and...

"Well?"

I clear my throat and shrug casually. "Because she's a sh— sucky witch."

The class laughs.

Griggs looks momentarily irritated but then recovers. "And your grandmother?"

Geez, read my file much?

"She's not sucky, just was a busy one. Relied on my mom to teach me, apparently."

I feel kinda weird talking about my personal life in here for some reason. I have a feeling it's going to be a long semester, and I need to just get over it. I'm sure every witch in this class is going to be under scrutiny at some point, and that we're all going to be divulging our personal shit.

"I see," he replies.

He points to the back of the class. "Mr. McLaughlin, what about you?"

I turn to see Jack from my Gym class. "Like Paige, I had sucky witch parents. They were fu—freaking ashamed to be witches. So they didn't teach me nothin'. Found out the hard way."

Knowing every one of us in here committed three

supernatural crimes, it makes me wonder what Jack and Alicia did. Like, had they used magic because they didn't know who they were or what they could do?

"Care to share what brought you to Larchwood?" Griggs asks him.

Is this truly an icebreaker session, or is he just trying to embarrass us? Break us? I stare into his face and I don't see any joy or malice there. He isn't exactly enjoying this, but he definitely has his proverbial instructor's hat on.

Jack shrugs. "Sure. Didn't know I could control people's moods and thought I was just plain lucky. I can get anyone to do anything I want just by touching them. Once I realized I was more than just lucky, I started experimenting on people. A little shoplifting here, a little nightclub VIP sneaking in. Dabbled in some unarmed bank robbery. Those cute bank tellers were like putty in my hands—"

"Okay, Mr. McLaughlin, that's enough." Griggs sighs.

"What? You asked," Jack replies.

"I'm aware, but you're supposed to be remorseful for your crimes, not proud of them."

Jack was being a little bit cocky in his answers, I'll agree with the headmaster there.

"I am remorseful. I should have never told that girl to jump off a bridge. I didn't think my power was that strong. I thought they were just suggestions. That was my final 'crime'." He puts up air quotes.

The class gasps.

Damn. Like Jory, he killed someone. I cringed.

"And that's why you're here. To learn how to master that. It's a gift, and you used it for malice."

"I know," Jack says. "She didn't die but now her whole family thinks she tried to off herself."

Glad she didn't die, but that still sucks.

"Does it only work on humans?" I ask Jack as I'm still turned around.

He puts his gaze on me and I watch his eyes flash purple, the way all witches' eyes do when they're doing something magical. "No." He slaps his hand on Astrid's arm and grips it. "Stick your tongue out at Paige."

Astrid obeys immediately.

"Holy crap," I breathe. I'm not sure if that's a gift or a curse. I can see how Jack would be tempted to do all kinds of bad things with that kind of power.

Astrid snatches her arm away and snaps, "Ew, don't do that again."

"Ms. Marx, how did that make you feel?" Griggs asks.

She puts her attention on the headmaster and looks as though she's trying to formulate an answer.

"Just be honest," I coax.

"Icky. Like I couldn't move, and my thoughts weren't my own." She looks at Jack. "I didn't like it."

Jack chuckles. "Noted."

"Thanks for the demonstration, but no more of that." Griggs measures Jack with a warning glare.

Jack nods once in acknowledgment.

"Anyone else care to share any special gifts they have, aside from just being a witch?"

Astrid raises her hand, and at Headmaster's nod, she says, "I can see auras."

"Is that so?" he asks. "What color is mine?"

"Blue," she answers immediately.

He smiles and I sort of melt. My God, this man is beautiful.

"What does that mean?" he asks.

Beaming again, Astrid quickly prattles off, "Trust, faithfulness, stability, power, intelligence."

"Kiss ass...trid," Jack comments.

I give him a thumbs-up. "Good save."

He winks at me.

"Ooh, do me!" I say, and then immediately regret it as the class laughs.

"We will go over auras later in the semester," Griggs quickly adds. "Thank you for the read, Miss Marx."

"You're welcome!" she chirps, and I resist an eye roll.

"Anyone else?" Griggs asks the class.

Alicia clears her throat and says in a meek voice, "I can manipulate liquids."

The whole class, including me, gasps. How freaking cool.

I'm sure Headmaster knows all of these things about every single witch in the room, but he continues on as if he doesn't. "Is that so? Care to demonstrate?"

She glances around the room and stops when she spots Griggs's coffee cup. She gets up, walks to the desk, and points to the cup. "May I?"

"As long as you don't spill it," he teases.

With a grin, Alicia hovers her index finger over the top of the cup and begins swirling it around. The brown liquid begins to twirl up in a funnel out of the cup. More gasps can be heard throughout the room—including mine. She slowly moves the funnel down back into the cup and presents it to the Headmaster on the palms of her hands as if it were a gift.

"That's amazing!" I blurt.

"I agree," Headmaster says, taking the cup from her.

Alicia takes her seat and I turn to her. "Girl, that was wicked! Teach me, sensei!"

She giggles and mutters a thank-you.

Griggs asks if there are any other talented witches in the room, and at his silence, he starts a very long lecture on the history of witches and witchcraft.

Chapter 2

I sit back in my seat in the cafeteria and fold my arms over my chest. "Then spill it."

Astrid looks a big chagrinned as she twirls her spaghetti around her fork. "Why?"

"Because that whole aura thing was just bull…crud."

She pauses her noodle-twirling and looks at me with one eyebrow cocked. "It's not bull. It's real. I just may or may not have been telling the whole truth about his color."

We'd been having a discussion about auras at dinner, and when I asked her to elaborate on the headmaster's blue aura, she acted weird. I was currently interrogating the truth out of her.

"Then enlighten me. We're going to be learning this sh…stuff anyway, so let me get a leg up." I put my pinky finger to my mouth and raise one eyebrow, "Throw me a bone, Astrid."

She laughs and shakes her head. "You do a horrible Dr. Evil."

I nod. "Yep, I know. Spill the tea."

She sighs. "His aura was actually so dark, it looked black. In my defense, it could have been a really dark midnight-blue."

"So, what is black?" I ask, picking up a piece of garlic bread and taking a bite.

Astrid looks apprehensive, then blows out a breath, which causes a stray strand of light-brown hair to fly off her face temporarily. "Bold, rich, mysterious, elegant, strong, and…"

At her pause, my eyes go wide. "What? What else?"

She chews the side of her lip. "Evil."

I throw my head back and laugh. "The dude is hot. He's a little stuffy. And he's probably all those other things. But he's not freakin' evil, silly!"

She shrugs and finally puts the forkful of spaghetti into her mouth.

I feel strong hands on my shoulders before hot breath fans my neck. "What's happenin', hot stuff?"

I turn around to see scorching-hot dragon shifter Jory standing behind me. I grin up at him. "Takes one to know one."

He drops a quick kiss on the top of my head and leans down to whisper in my ear. "I'll get ahold of you later." He leaves with a wink and my temperature skyrocketing.

I watch appreciatively as he saunters off. "I hate to see him go but love to watch him leave."

Astrid and Alicia giggle. We invited Alicia to sit with us for meals. She's so sweet and shy.

I notice vampire Breckon, trailing behind him. He doesn't say a word to me, only stares me down with those smoldering black eyes and those full lips I want to bite. I clench my thighs together. Breckon follows Jory out and I turn around to see Astrid staring at the trio—group of three in which I only noticed the two. Axel, her way-too-buff-for-a-genie djinn is trailing behind my dragon and vampire.

Mine.

Why do I keep referring to those two as belonging to me? I'm supposed to be just kickin' it with one of them. Two isn't proper. Right?

There has to be three...

Breckon's words ring in my head. What does that even mean? Confrontations don't give me answers and I still don't know what to make of the statement. How can I be with two guys at once, let alone three?

"Earth to Paige."

I look over at my bestie and blink a few times. "Sorry. What?"

"Why couldn't he have kissed me like that?" She pouts at Axel's retreating figure.

I shake my head to clear it of all inappropriate thoughts and respond, "I don't know, but that boy should pay more attention to what his hot friends are doing. How to keep the girl and all that."

"Djinns are weak, that's why."

Astrid and I look up to see the redheaded bitch, my number-one nemesis Eliza, walking by with her tray on her way to the door. She gives us both a cool grin before depositing her trash in the receptacle and setting the empty tray on the top of it.

Astrid opens her mouth to retort, then shuts it again. After the succubus and her two cronies disappear through the doorway, I look at my bestie. "She's such a toad."

"Where was your witty retort? Your smartass remark?" Astrid asks.

We both pause and wait for Fembot to take points from her, but the horn sound never comes.

"Sweet, at least we know we can say 'smartass'."

"Beside the point," Astrid huffs.

"True. And to answer your question, I don't know. Bi…wench caught me off-guard."

Alicia snorts. "Yeah, you were too distracted by the dragon and vamp."

"You're not wrong," I reply dreamily.

"But seriously, why can't Axel be like that with me? Maybe he's just not that into me."

I get up and pick up my tray from the table, and Astrid and

Alicia do the same. On our way to the trash receptacle, I say, "He could be just shy. Maybe he's a virgin. Who knows?"

I say this because he still hasn't made a move on her, despite his swagger and seriously hot body. I'd ogled it several times while watching swim practice. The guy is all muscle, close to six feet tall, and has beautiful eyes. I'm not sure why he's pussyfooting around with my friend, but if he doesn't seal the deal soon, he may lose Astrid. She wasn't shallow, but he wasn't exactly making her feel wanted.

"Are you putting out the vibe?" I ask as we enter the Grand Hallway on our way to the female dorms. "Bye, Alicia," I say to her.

"Bye," she replies with a little wave as she heads for a different door.

Astrid puts her hand to her forehead and shakes her head. "I don't even know what that means."

Deciding we need to have this conversation somewhere more private, I grab her hand and lead her to the end of the Grand Hallway, scowling once at the Final Five rules posted at the top of the doorway, and out into the courtyard that will lead us into the female dorms.

"Are you serious?" I stare at her incredulously. "You're twenty years old."

Astrid huffs and rises from her bed to the bookshelf. There, she pulls down *War and Peace* and plops it onto the bed. "Are you trying to make me feel worse than I already do?"

Fuck.

"No! God, no. I'm just surprised, that's all. Plus, have no filter."

Astrid pulls out her spellbook from its hidden cutout of the big book and flips it open. I can't imagine she's in much of a mood to do magic, so I suspect she's trying to deflect.

Deflection doesn't work with me, though.

"I didn't mean to make you feel bad," I continue. "And really, there's nothing wrong with it. Nothing at all..." I trail off.

She looks down at her spellbook and licks her fingers once to wet the corners of the pages before continuing to flip. She doesn't look at me or acknowledge what I've said.

I walk over to her bed, slide her book away, and sit down. "Look at me."

Astrid gradually lifts her gaze to mine. She looks sad and oh-so innocent.

"There's nothing wrong with being a virgin. I'm just surprised is all. I was wrong with my reaction, and I apologize."

Her lime-green gaze searches mine for a minute before she nods slightly and then licks her lips. "Okay."

I give her a quick hug and walk back to my bed on the other side of the room. "I think it's pretty awesome, actually. You and Axel both all shy and virginal. It's gonna make for one explosive first time."

She tries to act angry, but I can see she's biting back a smile. After an exaggerated huff, she says, "I guess you're right."

I open my side-table drawer and pull out a nail file. "You know what you and Axel should do? Just wait. No need to risk the B.S. punishment here for breaking 'rule number four' with the sexual contact ban."

She laughs. "It's funny you say that, because we've actually talked about that."

I pause the nail file on my middle finger and look over at her. "You have?"

She nods and looks down at her spellbook. "I know I said I was frustrated earlier... and don't get me wrong, I am. But I've learned over the past few weeks that it's because he's shy... like me. Just gonna have to take things slow with him."

"That's not a bad thing," I say, meaning it, and silently wishing I hadn't been so loose and carefree in the past of couple years. "Seriously."

"I know. I just never thought, in all my wildest dreams, that my life would have taken this turn. I never thought I'd end up locked away in the mountains of Montana for some stupid crime I didn't even mean to commit. It's just so unfair." She sighs dramatically.

"I didn't either, girlfriend. I didn't either. Who knew this crazy place even existed?"

"I certainly didn't," Astrid mutters under her breath as she flips through the spellbook.

I watch her continue to flick through her book and get jealous that she even has hers. I need mine badly. I have so much regret not studying and memorizing mine to a tee. "I need my book," I say, blankly staring at hers.

"Yes, you do." Astrid nods in agreement. "Until we can figure out a way to hijack it from Griggs, I need you to help me on a spell to quell this sexual frustration. It's making me insane."

I jab a thumb toward the bathroom and say, "Well, I still haven't ruled out the idea of using the hairdryer motor to make a vibrator. If you want me to rig you up one, just let me know."

Astrid laughs and nods. "I'm thinking I'm gonna have to take you up on that here very soon."

Chapter 3

Technically, girls aren't allowed in the boys' dorms, and vice-versa. But it's not like they have security roaming around to enforce that rule. I know there are cameras mounted outside the dorm buildings, and in the hallways, but there are ways around that. I also know that's how Jory got caught in my room by Griggs a few weeks ago. Now that I'm in their room—since Breckon and Jory are roommates—I know we should be fine. Breckon loaned me his Academy hoodie yesterday and then, once I was inside the building, turned all the lights off in the hallways so I could sneak in quickly.

After ushering Breckon inside, he closes the door behind us, and it's on.

He wastes no time slamming me up against the door and quickly relieving me of the hoodie. He throws it on the ground and then devours my mouth with his. Our tongues mingle together while we paw over each other like a couple of teenagers.

Okay, technically, we are, but I'll be twenty in a couple of months and I think he will too. I'll have to ask him when his birthday is when I'm less horny and can think straight.

"When will Jory come back?" I ask quietly between kisses.

"After midnight. Coach is busting our balls for some shit that happened in the locker room earlier this week. I faked sick so I could see you." He looks down at me and grins. "Now stop asking questions and get your fine ass on my bed so I can see that pussy."

The rebel in me wants to protest but there is no use since his commanding nature is turning me on. I do as he says and I'm glad Fembot can't hear our forbidden words while in our dorms because I have a feeling I'm about to cuss up a storm here in a bit.

I didn't wear anything under the hoodie, so I quickly slip off my gym pants and lay down on his bed. Breckon reaches behind him and pulls his gray T-shirt off over his head, and I unabashedly let my gaze roam over his sexy chest.

He's too busy watching me, his stare raking me from head to toe. "So fucking beautiful," he says and then prowls over to me with predator precision.

Sitting next to me, he stares into my eyes while he runs his finger over my lips and then inserts one into my mouth. I suck on it automatically and he hisses out a quiet breath. "Damn, baby."

I grin around his finger and he pulls it out with a pop. He slowly begins running it down my chin, throat, and then to my left nipple, which causes a jolt of pleasure to travel straight to my core. Both nipples are tight buds, and when Breckon leans down to capture one in his mouth, I moan almost climax right there.

Careful not to ignore the right nipple, he lavishes some attention on that one too before kissing his way back up to my mouth and devouring it once again. I rake one hand through his midnight-black hair and then slither the other down to reach outside his sweatpants to feel what he's working with.

Oh, my...

He's hard as a rock and very endowed, and I can't wait to play with it. I shiver when he groans against my lips.

He continues to kiss me, and I feel like I'm going to explode before he even touches me. With my head lolled back in pure ecstasy, I miss the fact that we are now lying side by side on the bed instead of sitting up. When he slides a finger inside me, I gasp in pleasure and surprise. He breaks the kiss and pulls his finger out of me, trails it up my slit, then my stomach, and then puts it in my mouth.

"Suck your juices off," he commands. I obey and find it surprisingly erotic and not as gross as I thought that would be after reading about it in books. When he tears his sweatpants off and tosses them to the floor, I'm mesmerized by his cock springing free. He is on his knees on the bed now, and I want nothing more than to put my mouth on his dick. I stroke it a few times and he hisses in pleasure at my touch. That makes me feel powerful and sexy, so I slowly lean down and take all of him into my mouth.

"Oh, my God," he groans. He grabs my hair and begins controlling my head as I bob up and down. I've heard other girls say they hate that. I find I don't. I like his commanding touch and while he's not hurting me, he's using just the right amount of pressure to control me, yet lets me take the lead.

"You need to stop, Paige," he pants out, and then pulls my head back by my hair.

I pout up at him. "But you taste so yummy."

He slaps my cheek like he did before, and I groan with a smile. "Quiet, no talking."

I nod in agreement before he reaches over and kisses where he'd slapped, then rubs it with his thumb. It didn't hurt (that much) but I appreciate the soothe of his mouth and fingers, nonetheless.

He bites back a grin and pushes me down on the bed. Kissing me briefly once more, he trails his hot mouth down my body, lavishing my breasts for a little bit until I can barely stand it, and then kisses down until he reaches my soaking wet core. He runs a finger through the juices before shoving two fingers in this time. "You're going to scream, so use the pillow. I don't need any interruptions."

I raise an eyebrow at him but then slam my head back when his mouth clamps onto my clit. His fingers are still inside, stroking my g-spot, and I'm almost embarrassed at how fast I come with just a few sucks and licks of his talented mouth. He was right about the pillow; it was very useful.

I have barely caught my breath when he's suddenly on top of me. I can feel his thick head probing my wet and throbbing entrance, and I suddenly stiffen up. "Condom," I pant.

"No, baby. We don't carry diseases and I can't get witches pregnant."

Remembering we discussed this in Occult Studies, I know he's right.

"Okay," I breathe, staring up at him. I watch in fascination as his fangs descend. Without my permission, he leans down and inserts them in my neck. I'm not afraid this time because I know the pleasure comes shortly after the very small pinch of pain.

His cock enters me at the same time his fangs do, and I want to scream again at the sensation. I buck my hips slowly to meet his, the bundle of nerves between my legs swollen and needy for another release. I gasp at each powerful thrust, my body on sensory overload at the feeling of him inside me, his fangs pulling my life force into his mouth, his moans near my ear. When he drags his fangs out and kisses me, I taste my own blood, but it doesn't bother me. He pulls up on his hands and stares down at me, his fangs still out, and then rears down to suck on my nipple. I watch in fascination as he inserts the tip of one fang into my sensitive areola and then licks the blood there. I almost climax just watching the ecstasy on his face as he licks and shudders.

Breckon continues to pump in and out of me, and with his powerful thrusts, combined with the suckling at my breast, I reach for the pillow and scream out an orgasm of which I've never experienced before. It's like my mind, body, and soul are coming together, meeting as one. With my eyes closed, I see stars explode behind my eyelids, and it takes me several minutes to wonder if anyone heard my scream.

I want to collapse in a boneless heap, but Breckon's deliciously punishing thrusts against my hips quicken, his breaths urgent. With the junction between my legs still sparking with sensitivity, I find I'm quickly working my way to another climax, his jerking movements making me see stars again. With one final thrust, he stills inside me and I soar high once again, the orgasm to end all orgasms rendering me weak and boneless. I lie completely vulnerable under this vampire who has done what no other boy—man—has done for me in all of my short adult life.

"You're so fucking beautiful," he whispers in my ear before collapsing on top of me in a warm heap of flesh and emotions.

I sigh in the most girly way possible, my limbs still tangled around his hard, sexy body as if he's my lifeline. "I'm glad you think so, my sexy vamp." Then, I lean up and kiss him hard and fast on the mouth.

After a few minutes of rest, we reluctantly dress, and I figure Breckon's going to tell me to leave. But he surprises me with a searing kiss and a sensual whisper in my ear. "This was fun I hope we can do it again. Maybe in your dorm next time, you little minx." He bites my bottom lip playfully with his regular teeth.

Dressed in his sweatshirt and my gym pants, I grin at his words. With the hoodie pulled up over my head, I slowly make my way out of his dorm, but not before he shut the lights off. Once I reach outside, I take a cautious look both ways to make sure no headmaster is around, spying on me. Not that I think he would be, but all the damn rules and regulations around here have made me a bit paranoid. Being caught out on one very embarrassing occasion is enough for me.

I look both ways down the massive hallway and pull the hood of Breck's sweatshirt over my face. I don't see any hidden cameras, but I know they're in here.

"Hurry up," I hiss to Astrid, who's carving runes on the palm of her hand.

"Stop it. I need to concentrate," she snaps back in a whisper.

We are going to be in so much trouble if Griggs finds out we're trying to break into his office. But I need my damn spellbook.

I watch in fascination as the rune on Astrid's hand glows a faint purple for just a couple of seconds. She presses it to the lock, and I hear it click open.

"Holy crud," I breathe.

She pushes the door open and we sneak inside. I spy Yvette's desk, everything neat and in its place, and then look to where Griggs's office is. The door is closed.

"That better not be locked, too," Astrid comments, heading toward it. "I'm already feeling drained, and honestly, a little guilty, for busting the lock on the door to the office."

"You're a great friend," I say, clapping her on the shoulder.

She snorts and puts her hand on the doorknob. It turns easily, fortunately.

Not risking turning on a light, I squint in the dark, trying to find anything that will give me the location of my personal belongings. Being that Griggs handed out our cell phones here, I assume the rest of our shit must be somewhere, too.

A massive bookcase sits behind his desk. I'm thankful for the full moon tonight, as its light streams in through the large window to the right of his desk. Astrid is trying to open his drawers, but they're all locked, save for the one in the center. It only seems to contain pens, pencils, and other random supplies.

I turn my attention back to the bookcase, when a certain book catches my eye and I inadvertently run my fingers over its spine. *A Case For Witches* is the title and I tilt my head, the spine mesmerizing me. But I don't know why. It's just a plain, dark-colored book with what looks like gold writing. My body suddenly heats up as if I have a fever and a spark flies from my fingertip. Next thing I know, the bookcase is sliding into the wall, and before us is a dark, empty space, inviting us to walk into it.

"Oh, my God," Astrid whispers under her breath. "Secret passageway." She tears her gaze from the big black space and looks at me with wide eyes. "Should we go in?"

I flick my eyes to her and grin. "Of course, we should."

Chapter 4

Swallowing hard, I grab Astrid's hand and step into the darkness. It's so damn pitch dark in here, I can't see my hand in front of my face. "I'd kill for a flashlight or even a lighter."

"Hold on," Astrid says quietly. She turns around and pulls something from Griggs's desk drawer.

A thin pillar candle and lighter are in her hands, and she quickly lights the candle and indicates for me to lead the way.

"Weird. Who keeps a candle in their desk drawer?"

"Or a lighter?" Astrid adds.

"Probably confiscated the lighter from a student," I reply.

We make our way in the darkness, candlelight our only illumination, and we don't have to walk far when we reach a set of stone steps leading down. At the bottom is a cache of items. Backpacks, purses, even black trash bags of stuff just strewn all over the place. Even with the candlelight, I can't tell what else is down here, so I waste no time locating my pink and white purse. I bite back a squeal before rushing over to it.

"Don't take the whole thing. Just get what you need out of it," Astrid instructs, chancing a glance behind her.

She's right. Don't make it obvious.

I open up the big shoulder tote and retrieve my spellbook, my favorite lipstick, my three-month pack of birth control pills, and the Swiss army knife I never went anywhere without. I put the purse back where I found it, and Astrid and I quickly make our way out of the hidden passageway.

With my precious items in hand, we scramble up the stone steps and make it back to Griggs's dark office without incident.

Astrid blows out the candle and replaces it and the lighter back in the desk drawer. We go to leave, but then realize I need to close the bookcase.

"Shoot," I mutter quietly. "I don't even know how I opened it."

"You don't?" Astrid practically screeches.

"Shh!"

I look for the book *A Case For Witches* and locate it easily. I touch it and nothing happens. "Hmph."

"What did you do to open it?" she asks, almost sounding panicked.

"I don't know! I just touched it and the dang wall slid back!"

Astrid looks toward the door again, her paranoia stressing me out. She looks at me, and from the moonlight streaming in through the window, I can see the panic in her face. "Just go back to the room. I'll figure this out," I tell her. No use in both of us getting jammed up if we get caught.

"No," she whispers. "We'll figure this out."

I nod and look at the book again. I'm still intrigued as to its contents but not sure how to make it activate like I had before.

"Concentrate on your magic. Reach inside you, Paige." Astrid's sensical words soothe me.

I close my eyes and reach a finger up, touching the spine. I don't feel the same rush I had before, and when I crack one eye open there's nothing happening. I start to feel anxious and frustration but remind myself those emotions won't do me any good right now.

"Concentrate, Paige. You got this. Reach down into your core and pull the magic from there. It's the only thing that's going to close this bookcase."

She's right. With one finger on the spine of the book, and my other hand pressed against my spellbook flush against my belly,

I close my eyes and release the breath I've been holding. I dig deep for any spell I can remember from my book and then realize how stupid I'm being. I literally have the spellbook in my hand!

I vaguely remember a spell I'd read that makes things bend to a witch's will. I then set the book on Griggs's desk and begin to flip through.

Astrid's hand lands on the book.

I look into her eyes. "What?"

She shakes her head. "You don't need the book. You opened the passageway without it. Find the magic within yourself, girlfriend."

She's right. I fucking got this.

I turn my back on my spellbook and face the bookcase. It feels like we've been sleazing around this office for hours now, but I know it's been mere minutes. I need to calm the hell down.

I place my hand on the spine of the book once more and close my eyes. I envision a ball of colorful magic swirling in my gut, waiting to be released. Then I envisage it flying up through my body, into my hand, and out my finger.

"*Claudere illud*," I quietly command it to close as a zap of energy releases from my finger. I open my eyes to see the book briefly light up in purple, lightning bolts crawling all over it like bugs. The bookcase begins to slide into place, and we don't even wait until it's all the way in place before we hightail it out of there. I'm sure to grab my spellbook from the headmaster's desk before we leave.

"How long do you think it's gonna be before he notices the book is gone?" Astrid asks me from her side of the room the following night. We've gone a whole twenty-four hours since the epic break-in and nothing has happened. Griggs didn't even seem to act weird in Magic 101 class today.

Do I feel guilty for stealing back my spellbook? No. I just have to be careful about what I do with it. Hiding it under my mattress is a safe spot for now, but I can't risk it being found in case they decide to do a random dorm search, so I'll need to find another spot for it. Using Astrid's logic, I search our bookcase for the biggest book on there.

My beloved Harry Potter book. The first one. It's huge and I could easily carve out the center like Astrid had done with *War and Peace* but I'm struggling with the ethics of it. That was the first book my grandma gave me. I was only about eight, still learning to read, but it had helped me excel quickly into advanced reading, and the magic and witchcraft in the story had drawn me in. I think she did that so it wouldn't be such a shock to learn not only that witches were real, but that we were actually ones ourselves. I do believe it had helped when I look back.

"What?" Astrid asks as she follows my line of sight. Then she smiles. "You gonna hide your spellbook in Harry Potter? That's a great spot. It's a huge book."

I look at her sorrowfully and explain my dilemma.

"Dang. That sucks. It's okay, we'll find you another book. I bet I could lift one from the library. Something boring and not sentimental."

I chuckle and get up from the bed. "I don't think stealing is gonna work. But I like the way you think."

Running my fingers along the spines of the dozen or so books we have stored there, I realize *The Sorcerer's Stone is* the only book big enough for a cutout to fit my spellbook. "I'll just have to find a different hiding spot," I finally relent. I can't defile the book that way.

"I don't blame you," Astrid agrees, then looks down at her

spellbook and picks up her Stile.

My eyes scan the room and land on the small dresser each of us was provided with the room. Hiding the book in my underwear drawer will be too obvious, but perhaps there's something else I can do. The chest is comprised of three long drawers. I don't have enough stuff to even fill all three, so the bottom one sits empty. I pull it open and find the bottom and sides are made of some kind of pressed wood. A good yank on it shows me two layers of the stuff. After retrieving my Swiss army knife from my mattress, I carefully cut out the first layer from the back of the drawer and set the long piece on the top of the dresser.

"That's gonna be really obvious if you hide it in there."

I look at my roomie and smirk. "Just watch the door."

Standing, I open the top drawer with all my undergarments, and smile at the variety of colors I now have to choose from thanks to the Kool-Aid packets. I grab all the garments and put them on the top of the dresser. I stare down at the empty space with my hands on my hips. I walk over to my bed, retrieve the spellbook, and set it up against the back of the drawer along with my knife. Then I take the cutout and press it against the contents. It stays in place for the most part but I'm going to have to find some nails or glue eventually to keep it in place. I toss the undergarments back in the drawer and close it.

"Come here."

Astrid walks over to me and I say, "Open the drawer."

She obeys and begins rifling through the garments. The piece of pressed wood in the back doesn't budge.

"Nothing to see here." She grins at me. "Good job."

"False back wall." I grin.

She bends down and opens the bottom drawer. She points to the cut out. "Well, it's obvious, if you're looking, that the back wall of this drawer has been messed with, but like I said, you'd have to actually look close to see that. I'd still shove some crap in here."

"Maybe I should paint it and say it was like that when I got it." I shrug.

"Good idea. Where you gonna get paint from?"

"I'll steal it from the Shop class, duh."

She chuckles and sits back on her bed. "So you'll steal paint but not a book?"

"Of course, because I'll just take what I need and leave the rest."

"Lights out, ladies and gentlemen," comes Fembot's disembodied nightly announcement.

I flip out the light, grab *Harry Potter and the Sorcerer's Stone*, and crawl into bed. Then I click on my small reading light they'd provided with the room and begin reading about the magic for about the hundredth time.

Chapter 5

Breathing in deeply, I close my eyes and inhale the fresh scent of the forest. Lodgepole and Ponderosa pine trees tower up all around us, and while it's cold out here, it's manageable. Yesterday, we were instructed to wear gym clothes to Magic 101 and meet in the parking lot for today's lesson. I barely slept last night, I was so excited to see what we were doing today.

I mean, the fact that I had my world tilted off its axis by a hot vampire has nothing to do with my sleeplessness. He rocked me to sleep just fine.

As we stand in a clearing, which looks as if it has purposely been made in the center of these trees, I look around. The pines are so tall I have to crane my neck all the way back to see their tops. Somewhere off to my right, I can hear water flowing, so probably a creek or maybe a small river of some kind. Mr. Griggs instructed us all to form a large circle, in which he now stands, and at its center is a small bonfire. He looks like a PE teacher in a tracksuit and V-neck T-shirt. He's only missing a whistle. Still riding my lusty high from last night, I let my gaze roam over his body and ogle his tight ass a little too long when he turns to face the other students across from me. He walks in a slow circle as he speaks.

"Some of you know this, some of you don't, but the first thing you need to understand about magic is that it comes from the elements. The water, the air, the earth, and lastly, fire."

I think back to how I threw that flame into Eliza's hair and am glad she isn't in this class for some awkward eye contact.

"Yes, Jack?" The headmaster points at him.

"So, each witch or warlock has power over one of these elements specifically?" he asks.

"Good question. Yes and no. As Alicia demonstrated last week, she's become quite skilled in water magic. Just like with humans and their gifts and talents, some witches will find they are partial to a certain element of magic." He looks directly at me. "Like Paige here. I believe she likes to dabble in fire magic. Isn't that right?" He dips his head toward the bonfire at his feet without breaking eye contact.

God, I wanna crawl under one of these big-ass boulders and hide. I clear my throat. "Uh, sure," I say. The whole school knows about my little display a few months ago. Even for the ones who weren't there, they sure got an earful of gossip over the following few days.

The students laugh.

"Do any of you have a partiality to any specific element?" Griggs asks, still walking in a slow circle.

"I've always been drawn to water, but I never tried to manipulate it. I always thought we were only good for doing spells and incantations. Sometimes a little palm reading and psychic stuff," one student comments. I can't remember her name but she's pretty quiet, and like everyone else, I briefly wonder what she did to get in here.

"Being raised by gypsies, that doesn't surprise me, Rainlily. In fact, it seems your parents knew you'd be drawn to water before you were born, just by giving you your unique name."

She nods. "They never taught me that we could manipulate the elements. I just know that I'm going a little stir-crazy being away from large bodies of water."

Griggs replies, "Yes, living in Michigan sure gives you lots of access to all those beautiful lakes and waterways, doesn't it?"

"Yes." She sighs wistfully.

"I promise we'll be near water soon, Rainlily." He throws her a wink that makes me irrationally jealous. He looks at the group. "Anyone else?"

He's met with silence, so the headmaster keeps lecturing. "Elemental magic has to be treated with extreme caution. You have to respect the element, or it won't respect you back. Give respect, get respect."

"What does that mean?" Jack asks.

Instead of answering, Griggs leaves the clearing and walks to a nearby tree. At its base is a single flower growing out of it. The yellow blossom looks lonely there on the ground, and I have the sudden urge to pluck it up. Some sort of organic beauty would bring a little bit of life to our dull dorm room.

I watch as the handsome headmaster closes his eyes and puts his hand toward the lone flower. Before our eyes, flowers of the same type begin to spring up from the ground, first as stalks, then as buds, then they blossom into full, yellow beauty. The metamorphosis happens within seconds, and before we know it, the gasping crowd is standing before what probably equates to a meadow full of flowers. They surround the base of the massive oak and stretch for yards ahead of us and all around us.

"Beautiful," Alicia breathes beside me.

But our awe is short-lived, as soon the earth under our feet begins to quake.

"Hold steady, feet shoulder-width apart, and ride out the tremors," Griggs yells in command to all of us.

Since there's nothing nearby to hold on to, I feel like I'm on a train with no 'oh shit' handle and do as the headmaster says.

The earthquake subsides as quickly as it appeared. Once I get my bearings, I breathe a sigh of relief. That sigh turns to a gasp as I see all the gorgeous yellow flowers have completely wilted and died. They lay lifeless and brown, and when a breeze comes along, the dead foliage is carried on the wind and the tree remains as it was before: Alone, aside from one yellow flower at its base.

"How in the f…freak did you do that?" I blurt, then wonder if

I can cuss out here since I doubt Fembot can hear me.

"I didn't, Paige," he responds quickly. "Recreate the circle, students."

"You created too many flowers," Alicia says quietly.

Griggs retakes his place at the center of the circle and smiles at her. "You are correct, Alicia. My power was overreaching and careless. What on earth do I need an acre-sized plot of flowers for? It angered the elements, threw off their balance. In return, I was punished with the demise of the foliage."

That makes sense.

Without leaving the circle, Griggs closes his eyes and puts his arm out. With his palm flat, he aims it toward the flower once again. We're a good twenty feet from the tree, but to my surprise, one more yellow flower grows, buds, and blooms before our eyes. He quickly walks to the new flower, plucks it up, and returns to the circle. Then, he heads over and hands it to Alicia. She smiles shyly as she takes it, then slides some dark hair behind her ear.

This also makes me irrationally jealous. I glance at Griggs and I don't miss the mischief in his eyes as he looks my way and holds my stare for a few long seconds.

That fucker did that on purpose.

Okay, cool. Two can play at that game. Maybe next time I'm in the lunchroom, I'll have my mitts all over Jory or Breckon. Or both. And he can watch it all on his precious cameras, to which I'll be giving eye contact as I do it. A devious smile finds my lips.

"What are you smiling about?" Astrid asks.

"Oh, nothing," I sing-song.

She shoots me a look that tells me she's going to quiz me later on it. I'm sure she will.

"So, do you all understand the nature behind respecting

magic and its limits now?"

A gaggle of yeses and hums of approval fill the clearing, but then something dawns on me. I raise my hand.

"Yes, Paige?" he asks, a stoic expression on his infuriatingly handsome face. He seems serious but the usual mischief in his blue eyes is there, as always.

"How did you make those flowers grow without using Latin?"

He nods once. "That's a very good question, young lady. Which brings me to my next subject." He begins walking in a slow circle again, but I'm irked.

Young lady? Seriously? Is this just a front he's putting on, or what? He obviously thinks of me as more than just a damn teenager or student, that's for sure. The proof is in the fact that he'd finger-blasted me just a few short weeks ago. I suppress a shudder at the memory. The lust in his eyes. His deep breathing. The straining erection in his pants. The quiet groan he'd emitted as his fingers found my swollen, wet core. The explosive orgasm he'd given me.

You'll have to keep this to yourself if you want more, baby girl.

Baby girl. Maybe he did have a bit of a fetish for younger women. But then again, just like I've been wondering, how old is this guy? He seriously can't be older than thirty. Maybe I should take to calling him 'daddy' like they do in those smut books I've read. That would probably drive him crazy.

"...but it's just not necessary. The use of Latin to perform magic on the elements died down decades ago. Latin is used in incantations of spells and certain tricks used by lesser witches." Griggs breaks me out of my musings with his continued lecture as he walks in circles.

Thank God I don't have to learn any more Latin. That shit sucks and hurts my brain. I guess my mom is a 'lesser witch' since she didn't teach me jack-shit about the elements. Only party tricks and circus magic. Which is what landed me in this godforsaken place to begin with.

That being said, I never had mind-blowing orgasms or hot-ass-hell supes chasing my tail like they do here. It must be the environment. They're stuck here, no girls to chase but us, so they put it down hard on us. I could be depressed by that thought, but instead, I realize that I'm doing the same thing. Finding the hottest guys at this Academy and having sex with them. It's against the rules, but then again, it's not like we're here in this prison disguised as a school for singing too loud in church.

Chapter 6

As I sit in Occult History, I can't concentrate on what Mr. Johnson is saying. I stare longingly out the window and wish we were still outside. Yeah, it's chilly, as March is pretty cold here in Montana, but it was just so refreshing to be out instead of in this stuffy classroom.

I'm also trying to distract myself from Jory and Breckon. They're both in this class and vying for my attention. I haven't even asked Breck if Jory knows that we hooked up. But something tells me he knows. The fact that Jory is still flirting and trying to catch my attention speaks for itself. As if he's getting off on it somehow. I expect alphas like him and Breckon to be pissed that I fucked someone besides them, but they don't seem bothered at all.

And why would they be? Breckon told me himself that he and Jory want to 'share me'. What does that even mean? The thought of the sexy dragon shifter and the smoldering vampire both touching me at once has me clenching my thighs together under the skirt of my uniform. What Breckon did to me a few nights ago still causes a blush to color my cheeks and my panties to dampen at just the thought. Is a *ménage à trois* with those two really in my future? What about a third?

I mull over my feelings. Am I developing feelings for one of them over the other? A hard contemplation tells me that no, I'm not. I want them both sexually, of course, but the sexy boys do cause butterflies to erupt in my belly. My heart races and a smile I can't control takes over my face at the thought of both of them. Is it possible to love more than one person at once?

Love.

I don't think it's quite there yet, but there are serious crushes and infatuation-like feelings going on. I love Jory's sweetness outside the bedroom and his attention to my needs inside it. The way he looks at me, holds my hand, asks me questions about myself. The way he stares at me, almost through me, as if he's expecting me to fall into his arms at just a look—and I want to. I also love Breckon's confidence and aggressiveness. The way he commands me to do things and then rewards me by showing me affection when I obey. I love the way he demands things but then looks at me questioningly while doing it, as if silently asking for permission. Even his punishments are erotic, and I wanted more and more of what he dishes out.

Snapping myself out of my inappropriate thoughts, I try to concentrate on the teacher. Unfortunately, we're covering Wendigos this week and the subject bores me. Mr. Johnson seems pretty passionate about the tall, emaciated supernatural cannibals, but I'm pretty disinterested. I don't believe in such creatures, and until I lay my eyes on one, I won't change my mind. Even if the folklore is deeply rooted in Colorado, my home state. I've lived there my whole life and have only ever encountered one other supernatural creature—the vampire my mother works for. Other than that, life has been pretty paranormal-free for me. Maybe I've been sheltered or maybe the other creatures I encountered had been hiding in plain sight as humans—just like we did.

As it stands, I now believe in not just vampires, but shifters, dragons, demons, and succubae, but that's it. The rest of the stuff Johnson is teaching seems to be so far out there. And I don't know why I find it so hard to believe when I know the other creatures exist, I just do. Even if I, myself, am one of them.

I try intently to listen to the rest of Johnson's lecture, and even to the questions the rest of the students ask, when of course a distraction comes sweeping in.

"Psst."

Johnson's back is to the class as he writes the Wendigo's characteristics on the board, so I chance a glance behind me.

Why do I keep sitting in the front of the class? That is so not like me. I see both Breck and Jory sitting next to each other and smiling at me. I flick my gaze between them both and furrow my brow.

"What?" I hiss, biting back a grin, then glance at Johnson quickly before turning my attention back to them.

"Check your phone," Breck mouths to me.

I shake my head. "Not in class, you psycho!"

He chuckles under his breath and we all straighten our postures and face forward when Johnson turns back around.

He continues to drone on about the creatures, all the while my damn phone is burning a hole in my messenger bag. What the hell is so important they had to send it to my phone? Being here isn't like being on the streets. I rarely use the thing due to the close contact we have with each other and the lack of need for the device due to having nowhere to go.

The bell rings and I hop up out of my seat and collect my bag. I hightail it to the bathroom, Astrid hot on my heels.

Once safely inside, I pull the phone from my bag and bring up a text from Breck. It's a photo of him and Jory, wearing only shorts, their muscular chests and stomachs shiny with sweat. They're pointing at the camera and a large printed caption at the bottom reads: "We're looking for one good woman to fulfill our every fantasy."

I swallow hard and jump when Astrid gasps from over my shoulder.

"Holy crap, that's hot!" she exclaims, staring down at the phone. "You should make that your screensaver." She slaps her hand over her mouth, and then is relieved when robo-bitch keeps quiet.

I chuckle. That would be awesome. Obvious, but awesome.

"You're one lucky girl." She sighs dreamily.

I stare at the smoking hot photo one last time, reply with a love-eyes emoji and a flame emoji, and then slip the phone back into my bag. "So are you, though," I reply, making my way toward the bathroom door.

"How do you figure?" she asks, following me.

"Your djinn still not wanting to seal the deal, or what?" I ask and realize that sounds kind of harsh.

She sighs dramatically as we exit the bathroom. I sling my arm around her shoulders.

"It's not that. I just wish he'd be more forward. Like your guys."

"I know you decided to do the abstinence thing for now, but it doesn't mean you can't do other things. Take the lead if he won't."

She stops walking and looks up at me. I'm only about two inches taller than her but it's still funny to see.

"I don't know. Maybe."

We stroll into the gym and I remove my arm from her shoulders as we make our way to the lockers to change.

"What element is it when you can see the future and read minds?" a boy from class asks.

All heads whip in his direction at the question.

"Who the hell is that?" I whisper in Astrid's ear.

We're again in the forest, standing in a circle in the clearing, small bonfire roaring, when a guy I've never seen before asks the showstopping question.

"I don't know. I saw him in class on Monday, but he never

says anything," she replies quietly.

Could have fooled me. I swear I've never seen this dude before. Probably because I've been too busy ogling a bunch of other dudes.

I stare at the guy. He's average-looking. About five-nine, light-brown skin, short, curly light-brown hair, full lips. Looks to be mixed Black and White maybe.

"Care to elaborate, Caleb?" Griggs asks.

He lifts a shoulder and lets it fall. "What's there to elaborate? I see shit before it happens. I can talk to people without speaking. It sucks and I'm fucking tired of it."

I like this guy already.

No loud horn strikes the air. No robo-bitch docks him any points. *Yes!*

"Watch your language, young man. Now, please provide the class with an example." Griggs nods at the student.

Caleb plunges his hands into the pockets of his track pants, nods at the tree, and shrugs. "I knew those flowers were gonna die."

Griggs walks over and stands directly in front of him. He peers down at Caleb, as he's got a good three to four inches on the student, and says, "Please elaborate."

"Please get the fuck up out of my space," was Caleb's only response.

I really, *really* already like this guy. I stifle a snicker.

Griggs's jaw tics in response, but then he nods ever so slightly and takes a step back. "In respect of your space, I have backed up. Minding your language, please continue, Mr. Owens."

Caleb eyes the headmaster speculatively, and then looks at us. His gaze locks on mine for a few seconds longer than socially appropriate, then moves on to the rest of the students. It eventually lands on Griggs before he says, "I had a dream, night before last. A field full of yellow dahlia flowers. I was walking through them, their fragrance amazing, when all of a sudden, they began to wither and die. Once they had all crumbled, and their remains were carried on the wind, I looked up to see you standing in the breeze, your arms folded across your chest. The look on your face was both triumphant and murderous."

My mouth hangs open, jaw unhinged. Not only am I surprised by the formality of his speech, especially after how he'd talked to Griggs just a few seconds ago, Caleb has just figuratively handed Griggs his ass for destroying those flowers.

"How you like me now?"

I jolt at the question. Glancing around the circle, nobody seems to be looking at me except Caleb.

"I like you very much," I reply, only inside my head, feeling weird but not completely wrong.

"I like you, too. You're a spicy witch." His mouth twists up into a grin.

Holy crap! This dude just talked to me. Inside his mind. Inside *my* mind!

"Earth to Paige!"

I look down to see my bestie staring up at me in confusion. "Oh, yeah. Sorry about that."

"I thought I lost you there for a minute," she says with a questioning gaze searching my face.

"You did," I reply. "We'll collab later."

"Collab. You got it." She rolls her eyes at my slang.

Headmaster Griggs cleared his throat and replies, "You're connected to the air. People's thoughts. Their feelings, their despair. Their hopes and their dreams."

"So I'm drawn to air magic, just like Alicia is drawn to water magic and Paige is drawn to fire magic?"

Griggs nods. "Yes, that's correct."

Caleb puts his hands on his hips. "And what magic are you drawn to, man?"

The headmaster narrows his eyes and replies, "I'm not drawn to a specific magic, but I've made it my goal to master in them all. And you'll address me as Mr. Griggs or sir. Not 'man'."

I want to laugh. What a cocky asshole. "Prove it," I blurt.

Headmaster Griggs thrusts his hands into the pocket of his athletic pants, a very stiff maroon pair with a yellow stripe down the side—school colors—and tilts his head at me. With an almost-smirk on his lips, he says, "I don't have to, Paige."

"You don't have to, but we'd like to see what you're workin' with. Sir." Caleb shoots me a knowing look. I throw him back a wink, and I swear Astrid's BFF status might be in question at this point. I already love this dude.

The interaction doesn't go unnoticed by Griggs, and the murderous look of jealousy that overtakes his features is frightening. Without a word, he waves his hand toward the bonfire, closes his beautiful blue eyes for a minute, and before anyone's aware, the tree with the lone dahlia flower are now fully engulfed in flames.

Chapter 7

The gasps and yells around me show me the students are frightened, but Griggs's actions aren't alarming me at all. I know he has a plan because I already know the slick headmaster better than I should.

With the tree still ablaze, he stalks off south, toward the sound of the rushing water that's never left my ears, and returns mere moments later, a huge ball of water swirling above his palm. As soon as he's within eyeshot of the group, he flings the water at the tree, and the fire subsides.

Griggs scans the group and then says, "Rainlily, Alicia, come with me." They obey, eventually disappearing behind a cluster of trees.

Another few long seconds go by and the trio emerges into the clearing with big balls of swirling water hovering above their palms.

"One, two, three…" Griggs isn't even finished saying 'three' before the trio hurls water at the problem.

The fire is promptly extinguished, and the crowd gasps.

The lone yellow dahlia remains intact, completely unscathed by the flames.

That's one magical fucking flower.

"You didn't respect the fire," Alicia comments quietly to Griggs.

He claps his hands together a few times to expel the excess water from them, and then looks at her.

I'm proud of her for speaking up because I was about to say the same thing about the way the tree became so involved so quickly.

"You're correct, Alicia. I didn't respect the element. That's how the fire became so out of control," Griggs responds.

My arms folded across my chest, I ask, "Why didn't you respect it? I mean, that's pretty dangerous. Sir."

"Don't worry, I had it under control, Paige. I was just showing you what can happen if you let your emotions control your magic. In my case, you pissed me off with your attitude, so I threw caution to the wind, quite literally, and flung a spark at the tree."

I raise my eyebrow as the class gasps. "Uh, sorry I pissed you off."

"Apology accepted."

I scowl at him.

"Now, here's some controlled elemental magic." He again waves his hand toward the bonfire, closes his eyes, and I watch as a single flame dances on his palm. It doesn't burn him, in the same way the one I used on Eliza hadn't burned me. Opening his eyes, he walks to about six feet from the tree, flings the flame at the base, and closes his eyes once again. A small, controlled bonfire sits next to the lone dahlia and the tree does not go up in flames like before.

"Wait a minute… isn't the ground wet from extinguishing the flames?" I ask.

Griggs nods. "Yes, it was. I commanded the fire to dry the ground before it created the bonfire."

"Whoa," Astrid breathes next to me. "That's amazing, sir."

"So… you say the incantation in your head, doesn't have to be out loud?" Caleb asks, arms crossed.

"Correct, nor does it have to be in Latin, like we discussed yesterday." He looks at Rainlily and Alicia. "Put the fire out. Please."

They both nod, head to the water source, and return quickly

with balls of water. It really only takes one to put the fire out.

"Paige, do what I just did." Griggs stares at me.

I swallow hard "What? No. I can't."

"Yes, you can."

I slowly nod. "Okay." I don't think I can be that controlled. Case in point: Eliza's hair.

With a deep breath, I go to stand in the center of the circle, next to the bonfire. Griggs stares at me expectantly. I look at the fire, then my hand, then him.

"Go on," he urges.

I shake my head. "Okay, well I know how to fling fire at the tree, I just can't be sure it's not gonna go up in flames."

"It won't. You got this. Concentrate on the magic inside of you, then let the fire know you're in control. Grab a spark, turn it into a flame."

I whoosh out a breath, close my eyes, and concentrate. Once I feel relaxed enough, I open my eyes and stare at the bonfire. I'm mesmerized by its blue base and the tiny orange sparks that fly into the air and dissipate into nothing. I put my hand out and command one of the sparks to jump into my palm. To my surprise, it obeys. A small spark turns into a dancing flame, like the one on the wick of a candle.

"Very good. Now create a bonfire with it."

Nodding, I carry the flame to the base of a different tree and flick my fingers toward the base. Fire begins to engulf the trunk and roots. "Shit," I murmur.

Griggs puts his hand on my shoulder, and I resist a shudder at his touch. "It's not too late. Show the fire who's boss."

Putting out a hand toward the inferno, I pull magic from my core and say inside my head, *Calm and contain. Small fire. Don't harm the tree.*

The flames recede and gather into a tiny circle at the base, just how I'd envisioned when I'd commanded it to do so.

I squeal and clap. "I did it!"

Griggs quickly removes his hand from my shoulder, and I hate to admit it was his strength that helped me accomplish the feat.

I can't wait to tell Jory and Breckon what I did today!

Wait... Why will they care?

"Okay, good job, Paige. Now, extinguish the flames."

Huh?

I tilt my head at him. "How?"

"Figure it out." He folds his arms across his chest.

Panic starts to rise up in my throat and I have no idea what he's talking about. I can't manipulate water. I certainly can't just command the flames to die. Can I?

He jerks his chin toward the small fire. "You better hurry up."

I can see that my perfectly controlled bonfire is now starting to involve the tree, no doubt becoming erratic, just like my emotions.

"Fuck," I mutter. I grab Alicia's arm and say, "Show me the water source."

She wastes no time dragging me through a small path in the woods where a stream awaits us. She closes her eyes and commands some water to leap onto the palm of her hand. The flow of water is connected to the stream and begins to form a big ball.

"How the hell..."

"Close your eyes, tell the water what to do."

I obey, closing my eyes with my hand held out toward the

stream.

Bring yourself to me, I chant over and over in my head.

I crack an eye open and nothing is happening. No water is flowing into my hands from the stream.

"You better hurry up, Paige!" I hear Griggs yell.

I turn around and flip him off, even though he can't see me through the trees.

Alicia chuckles and says, "That isn't going to do you any good. Find your magic and tell the water to obey you."

Nodding, I close my eyes and put my palm out. "Come to me, dammit!" I say aloud.

"That won't work, trust me," she says softly, placing a hand on my shoulder.

I suddenly remember Astrid's words from when we were in Griggs's office stealing back my spellbook. I calm down and pull in a deep, cleansing breath while surrounded by the fresh air Mother Nature has provided us. Concentrating on my core, I envision the magic swirling there, and then direct it out of my fingertips to the water. Then, I realize this is the same as I'd done to the fire, just in a rapid-fire motion.

Come to me. Be one with me.

I pop my eyes open when I feel a splash of liquid on my palm and grin when it forms a small tidal wave curl at my command. *Let's go, we have work to do.*

Without a word, Alicia and her water-ball follow me back to the tree, which is quickly becoming engulfed, and we shoot the water toward it. It doesn't extinguish all the flames, so I put both hands out, shooting the water like laser beams toward the tree. Once the flames are out, I gasp in surprise to see the water trailing behind me, still tethered to its source like a leash.

Thank you, water goddess. You may rest now.

The water recedes and I breathe out a sigh of relief.

Shaking the water from my hands, I turn to face the headmaster and my fellow students. I'm met with open-mouthed stares.

Except Caleb. He's grinning. *"Spicy witch,"* he says inside my head.

"Thanks, Caleb." I wink at him.

"Holy crap that was amazing!" Astrid said, patting me on the back.

"Indeed," Headmaster Griggs responds, smiling.

Feeling a little weird with all the attention, I quickly sling my arm around Alicia's shoulders. "This girl here is who you should be thanking. She grounded me, helped me find the magic inside me. I was legit panicking. It was pretty scary."

Alicia's face flushes pink and she looks down at the ground without saying a word.

"While Alicia is clearly talented, and has had years of practice, this was your first time, Paige. You did amazingly well."

"Well, I had amazing help." I dip my head against Alicia's, and she grins.

"Agreed."

"Now, who's next?"

Chapter 8

I gasp and squeal as I exit the headmaster's office, looping my arm through Astrid's. "I can't believe it!"

"Me either, you potty mouth!" she agrees.

I let go of her arm and run as fast as I can down the Grand Hallway before flipping a back handspring originally intended as a cartwheel. I land on my feet, crouching to let my knees absorb the shock. After putting my hands up in a Y above my head, I yell out, "Yes!"

It's too bad this Academy doesn't have sports teams. I'd make a great head cheerleader.

We enter the cafeteria for lunch and stand in line to collect our bagged meal.

"What are you so happy about today?"

I turn to see Jory breathing down my neck and suppress a shudder at his closeness. Grinning, I turn and reply, "I have fifteen points."

His yellowish-green eyes peer down at me, and in them I see mischief dancing there. "Nice."

"Five more to go. I guess we've gotten a lot of points added for good behavior," I reply, a grin twisting up in my lips.

"Absolutely. We've been *very* good students."

Astrid juts a thumb at me. "But she had to go ask the secretary how many points she had. She can't do math, apparently."

I elbow her in the ribs. "Hey! It's not like I've been keeping a tally, unlike you. You nerd."

She shrugs. "There isn't very much to tally."

"True. Like I said, nerdy good girl. Unlike me," I snort.

I look up at Jory. Between the devious look on his face and his proximity, I'm starting to overheat. I suddenly lose my appetite and wish we were somewhere more private.

"Yes, we've been very good," he comments, licking his lips.

I flick a glance behind Jory to see Breck standing there, looking just as devious and delicious. If spontaneous human combustion were a thing, I'd be a charred skeleton right now.

Astrid clears her throat and I look at her to see it's our turn to grab our meals.

"We'll be in the courtyard, boys," I say, my bag held high in my hand.

Astrid, Alicia, and I make our way out the side door of the cafeteria and out into the courtyard that sits between the dining hall and the pool house. I try not to glance at the squat building and all the memories it invokes.

"So, like a month or two and you'll be able to get a weekend pass?" Astrid asks as she pulls a wrapped sandwich and chips from the brown paper bag. I hate the lunches here. I prefer a hot meal like breakfast and dinner.

"I think so? I should have asked Yvette how many points we earn each month with good behavior before we left the office."

"Well, I could probably do some quick math," Astrid offers.

I lift a shoulder and let it fall as I pull out a baggie of celery sticks and a premade container of peanut butter. "Go ahead."

"Later, when we're in the room and I can concentrate," she whispers.

I follow her line of sight to see Jory, Breckon, and Axel headed our way.

Axel goes to sit next to Astrid at the end of the bench and she's forced to scooch closer to me to make room for him. He hands her his paper sack so he can free a hand in order to sling it around her shoulders. I can almost feel the excitement and nervous energy coming off of her in waves.

My smoking hot dragon shifter and sultry vampire take a seat on the bench across from me, and I'm instantly jealous at the closeness Axel and Astrid have. Alicia stiffens next to me, probably nervous around the vampire.

Jory unwraps his sandwich and takes a bite of it without breaking eye contact with me. He's obviously less picky than I am, because I'd already inspected the sandwich inside and out to discover it's chicken salad—chopped almonds and celery inside.

I swallow the bite I'd just taken and ask Breckon, "So, how many points do you have?"

"Does it matter?" he asks around the mouth of the small water bottle included in our lunch sack.

"No, you ass…butt… I was just asking."

"He has eighteen, I have thirteen," Jory replies.

I look at Axel. "And you?"

He stares hard at me for a minute, his light-brown eyes are almost green, and I notice, for the first time, that he has wavy black hair. He looks to be mixed Asian and something else. He's quite striking and I can see why my bestie is enamored with him.

"Twenty," he replies.

"Don't let his rockstar name fool you. Axel's a total fu…fudging nerd." Breckon grins at me before popping a celery stick into his mouth.

I flick my eyes to the djinn and say, "Is that so?"

"Leave him alone," Astrid pipes up defensively.

"So, if you're both rockin' the points, why haven't you taken your weekend passes yet?" I ask, knowing that Astrid said she wanted to wait for me, but wondering what Axel's excuse is.

"I've got nowhere to go," Axel replies, piercing me with his intense stare.

"He's holding out for the witch," Jory says, looking at Astrid, then throwing me a knowing look.

"I know," I reply, rolling my eyes. "You don't need to be so blunt about it."

Alicia clears her throat.

"Oh, sorry. Jory, Breckon, Axel, you know Alicia? We have Occult History with her."

"Hey," and "What's up?" they say in unison.

I take a bite of my sandwich and after swallowing, I say, "Hey, guess what?"

The group stares expectantly at me. "I learned how to manipulate fire and water yesterday."

Breckon's sandwich pauses at his lips. "I bet Eliza would have liked to have seen you do them both together a few months ago."

Jory, Breck, Axel, and Astrid all giggle, and I smile, too, as he made a funny. But he isn't wrong—finding some water to put out her fire would have been handy.

Not that I think she would have learned anything had I done that. The girl is still a complete tool and I want nothing to do with her.

"So are you like a master at it now or something?" Jory asks.

I snort out a laugh. "Not in the slightest. I did learn some things, though." I jerk a thumb at Alicia. "This girl here, she's the master at water manipulation."

"Is that so?" Breckon asks, staring at her intensely.

She shrugs. "I guess."

"Mind if I join?"

We look up to see Jaxon, the demon headed our way. His almost-white hair looks extra pale with the sun beating down on us.

I feel Alicia stiffen next to me again. Clearly she's uncomfortable around other species. Or maybe it's just boys?

"Of course," Jory says, pointing to an empty bench.

He sits and stares at all of us, then his gaze lands on Alicia. "I don't think I know you."

"Jaxon, this is Alicia Vazquez. She's kinda shy." I smile.

"Cool, nice to meet you." He gives her a flirtatious smile.

She nods shyly and says, "Likewise."

"Now what were we talking about?" Jory asks.

"Points. I've got fifteen. I figure by July I'll be at twenty, as long as I behave. Then I can get out of here for my birthday."

"That sounds like fun," Jory says, waggling his eyebrows.

"Yes, it does," Breckon says under his breath and I catch his heated stare, even from behind his sunglasses.

I look up into the sky and see there are no clouds in sight and know he isn't going to last very long out here. He doesn't sweat but I can bet he's uncomfortable.

Still, he doesn't budge. Just sits and stares at me through his sunglasses and I wonder what's going on inside his mind. I mean, I can guess.

I break the stare-off and say, "Hey, what do you guys know about that Caleb guy? He's a warlock. Met him in Magic class. Never seen him before."

"I think he's new," Alicia pipes in. "I hadn't seen him before either. Just popped up a couple days ago. I think."

Being that Alicia is the silent observer type, I believe her.

"No idea who he is," Jory says, finishing the last of his

sandwich and putting all the trash into the brown paper sack.

"Whoever he is, he's pretty freakin' powerful," Astrid pipes in. "Can see the future and stuff."

"Are you serious?" Breckon asks.

I nod. "Yep. Or so he says. Possesses some kind of psychic thing."

"Probably a clairvoyant witch," Axel interjects, and it's only the second time I've even heard his voice.

"Really," I reply. "I know there are different types of witches, but I've never heard of any type having premonition dreams and them coming true."

He nods. "My mom's one. My dad's a djinn."

"Must have been hella freaky growing up with a mother who knew your every move before you made it," Jaxon inserts with a laugh.

I guess *hella* isn't a bad word out here. Huh, good to know.

"No, she didn't know my every move. She only had dreams about big events before they happen. Like when my grandpa died, and the day before nine-eleven."

"I don't think that's a gift I'd want," I say, shaking my head.

"Me either," Astrid inserts.

The bell rings, so we all gather our trash and head toward the admin building to attend our afternoon classes.

I've seen this building a million times but had no idea what it was. I thought it was probably some janitorial or supply storage. But it's actually the Practical Magic building. Not only do we get to take our classes in the forest, but it also seems Griggs has secured a secret building for us to do magic in. Once we're all standing outside with our backs to the building, he closes his eyes and waves his hand. After he opens them, he says, "Look."

We turn around to see a beautiful white building resembling a castle with the words *Practical Magic* written across the top. It's not an enormous place, but big enough, I suppose. It looks nothing like it does from afar, and when Griggs tells us all to head inside, I realize he's probably glamoured it from the non-witches on campus.

Well played.

The inside is about as big as a ballet studio, maybe a little bigger. The walls are painted black and there is a very large skylight cut into the ceiling, which is at least twenty feet high. There are no chairs or whiteboard, so I'm assuming this will be all hands-on.

"Please, students, form a circle," the headmaster instructs.

We do as he says, and he stands in the middle of the room. "As we've been learning in the forest the past few days, all magic comes from the earth. I explained that it was called elemental magic. Some of us are better at certain elements than others—and that's okay. I want all of you to be able to manipulate all four elements before you leave this Academy. And we will be going back out there, but more towards the summertime when it's warmer." He waves a hand around to the building and continues, "But for now, we are going to learn some fundamentals of practical magic here. The regular classroom is too small and stuffy for learning anything other than the need-to-know stuff, like the history of witchcraft and things like that. Here, we will be doing hands-on work."

A few "yeses" and cheers could be heard around the room. Who doesn't love learning hands-on?

I'd sure like to get my hands on…

"First of all, who knows what practical magic means?"

"It's a movie from the nineties."

I turn around to see Caleb standing there with his arms folded across his chest, a smile on his full lips.

"Funny," Griggs says dryly.

"Thanks," Caleb calls out.

I snort and say, "I assume it's the practical application of magic. Tangible things."

Griggs beams at me and I resist squirming under his intense blue gaze. "Very good. What kind of things?"

"Runes? Auras?" Astrid says, of course, because those are her favorite things.

Griggs nods. "Yes, Astrid. What else?" He looks at the class.

"Magic wands, broomsticks, pointed hats, cauldrons, black cats…" Caleb grins.

"*Hocus Pocus*. That's a movie from the nineties." Griggs replies smugly.

The class laughs. Smartass little warlock had that coming.

"Funny," Caleb parrots.

"Spells?" Alicia asks.

"Yes," Griggs replies. "And in learning spells, we'll be incorporating certain herbs and objects needed for said spells. Now, let's get started."

Chapter 9

"You're not supposed to hit girls," I say, faking pain on my upper shoulder where he good-naturedly punched me. I jut out my bottom lip in a fake pout just to drive the point home.

"You're a pussy…cat," Caleb says quickly to avoid robo-bitch taking any more points. "And if you don't put that away"—he stares at my protruding bottom lip—"I'm gonna put it away for you."

I stick it out even further in defiance.

Caleb reaches behind my head and pushes my face into his. His warm, silky lips embrace mine, and I swallow down a gasp of both excitement and surprise.

We're supposed to be watching the male swimmers. I never asked, but I got the impression Caleb's gay and want to make a good friend out of him, so the kiss is kind of a shock. He ate dinner with Astrid, Alicia, and me, and we agreed to meet here after dark to watch the swim team. Astrid claimed she had too much homework, and Alicia is too shy to leave her dorm for anything but food and classes, so here we are, just the two of us.

Caleb's hand slips up my arm and to my face where he caresses my cheek as he kisses me. I reluctantly break the kiss, and with swollen lips and breath I'm trying to catch, I say, "Well, that was a surprise. A nice surprise, but definitely not expected."

"Why not, spicy witch?" He grins at me, and I'm mesmerized by his perfect white, straight teeth. They're so perfect they should use them in toothpaste ads. Maybe it's the stark contrast against his warm-colored skin.

"I… I…" cannot get the words out.

"You thought I was gay," he states.

I nod once.

"It's cool. I'm bi. I'm mostly into dudes, but I don't turn down a girl when she hits on me."

I raise an eyebrow. "I wasn't hitting on you."

"I know." He grins.

"Well, you're a fu…fudging good kisser. I'll give you that."

I'm not lying. Jory and Breck kiss very well, but this guy's blowing my socks off.

"What's going on over here?"

We look up to see Jory and Breck standing by the bleachers. Both are shirtless with towels slung around their shoulders. We must have missed their laps during our makeout session.

"Jory, Breckon, this is Caleb. He's a warlock. New to the school." I look at him. "Am I right?"

Caleb rakes his gaze up and down the two boys and gives a sound of carnal approval before he says, "Yeah, babe. That's right. New here. And *ohhhh* so glad to be here."

Jory gives me a questioning look—no doubt confused by catching us making out and Caleb's very clear, flirtatious approval of the boys' physique.

"Caleb's bi."

Breck raises an eyebrow. "Is that so. And a witch?"

"That's right, man." Caleb stands and shakes hands with them both.

The dragon and vampire seem receptive to him, and I'm again surprised there doesn't seem to be much jealousy there. I don't know if I should be happy or sad about that.

Can't just one of them want me all to themselves?

Then I think about Headmaster Griggs. He seems to display a

little of the green-eyed monster when he sees me flirting with these boys. Maybe because he's older?

"Paige, meet us at our dorm room at midnight. Don't forget the hoodie," Breckon says, piercing me with this inky black stare. He looks at Caleb once more and says, "Good to meet you, man. Welcome to Larchwood."

Caleb grins. "Thanks."

As soon as the two hunky supes disappear into the night on their way back to the male dorms, Caleb grabs my face and makes me look at him. "Spill. Now."

I reach forward and peck him on the mouth with a grin. "Make me."

The warlock reaches behind my head and grips my ponytail. "Now."

His forcefulness is hot, and I'm not afraid one bit by his dominance, because I can see mischief dancing in his light-brown eyes. "Why do you even care?"

He jerks a thumb behind him toward the boys' retreating figures and says, "Am I gonna have to share you with those jocks?"

I lift my chin and say, "Yep," making the *P* pop.

Something between delight and surprise colors his features before he nods and smiles. "Hot. Very hot."

Staring hard at this beautiful boy for a few long seconds, I finally say, "What's with the guys at this school? Is monogamy dead?"

Caleb pulls me into his lap so I'm straddling him before he looks up into my face and replies, "Nah, it's not dead. But I think you're the witch they've been searching for. And if that's the case, you belong to them—to us."

"What in the f… frack does that mean?" I ask on a gasp.

Caleb ignores my question and whispers low, directly into

my ear to avoid Fembot's microphones, "So tell me, spicy witch, which one of those two have you let fuck you?"

Deciding that this guy likes surprises and bluntness, I put both hands on either side of his cheeks as I look down at him. "They both have beautiful cock…tails and know how to use them."

I feel Caleb stiffen against my core, which is pressed against him. "Holy shit, that's hot as hell," he whispers in my ear. "I may have to join y'all in the dorms tonight."

I make a *tsking* sound with my tongue and fake a Southern accent. "Now, I don't believe you were invited, kind sir."

It's Caleb's turn to pout. "Not nice."

"With what seems to be going on at this school, you'll probably have your turn with me," I mutter dryly.

He frowns. "Turn?"

I didn't realize how bad that sounded until I said it. "I mean… I thought monogamy the right thing to do, but I'm learning it most certainly isn't this school's jam."

"It's not just here. Men all around the world are beginning to learn that one perfect woman is worth sharing."

My eyes go wide. "I'm so far from perfect that—"

He silences me with a kiss that makes my toes curl. His cock throbs against my core, its only barrier my thin Kool-Aid dyed panties and his athletic pants.

As we continue to kiss on the bleachers next to the pool, I begin to hear a faint sound inside my brain.

"Goddamn, you're so beautiful, Paige. You're the one. I just can't believe you're gorgeous and perfect. I thought we'd have to search harder for you."

I'm tempted to break the kiss at the shock of hearing Caleb's confession in my head, but I continue kissing him, my fingers raking through his curly hair, my nails running down his neck.

He runs his hands down my neck and one lands on my breast, his fingertips gripping my nipple through the thin T-shirt I wear with no bra.

I whimper in pleasure, just wanting to strip his pants off and do him right here on the bleachers. The physical attraction to this guy is off the charts and I think of how I never dreamed coming to a correctional academy would bring out my inner hussy.

"What do you mean?" I ask. Inside my head.

Caleb breaks the kiss and then gently shoves me back onto the bleachers so we're sitting side-by-side once again. "We'll discuss it later."

He stands, adjusts his dick behind his pants as I watch in fascination—it is at eye level now—and then stares down at me. "You'll see. I promise."

He leans down and kisses the top of my head before sauntering off and out of the pool house.

Holy shit. What just happened?

"Are you going?"

I stare at Astrid, who's got her electronic tablet laid out on the bed, along with her spellbook. Her Stile is in her right hand and she's looking at me expectantly in our dorm room.

"Duh, of course I am." I zip Breckon's Academy hoodie up and pull the hood over my head.

"Must be nice," Astrid replies on a sigh.

Damn. Now I feel bad.

I walk over to her bed and sit. "I know you and Axel will seal the deal soon. He's a pretty quiet dude, but he also seems like he's really into you. I think you chose correctly, to be honest. Unlike me…"

She sets the Stile down and cocks her head at me. "What do you mean?"

I sigh. "I mean… these guys all want me… like, sexually. They've all implied it's some kind of fulfilled prophecy, but I don't understand. Every time one of them mentions it, I just ignore it, as if it's some kind of farce—some kind of lip service just to get me into bed. I don't know… I'm just… fu… fracking confused. I guess."

"Maybe you should listen to what they're saying." She slides some hair behind her ear.

"Why?" I ask.

She stares at me for a long, hard minute until her teeth find her bottom lip.

"Just spit it out, Astrid." I sigh.

With a shake of her head, she finally says, "I'm thinking that these guys are telling the truth."

I hiss out a breath that causes a stray strand of hair to blow up to the ceiling. "What?

"Anything I say from this point forward is gonna make me sound like a judgy bitch. But I'm not. You are pretty easy with these guys—you're confident, you know—which I can totally appreciate and am a little bit jealous of, honestly—so that makes me think that you're special to them. Not just because you're willing to give it up, but because they feel you're part of something bigger."

I can't with this double-speak. I love Astrid, but my confusion is revving. I head for the door. "Don't wait up." I throw her a wink to keep the peace and head out.

The jog to the men's dorms is a quick one, and with Breckon's hoodie pulled up over my face, I quickly gain access to the male dorm building. The lights in the hallways are out, and I know Breck arranged that. I quickly find his dorm and knock.

Chapter 10

Breckon answers the door in nothing but his boxer briefs, and I suck in a breath at the sight. Pale, muscular chest. Six-pack abs. Narrow, tapered waist that leads down to thick quads. My God, he's beautiful.

"Hey, baby."

He greets me with a searing kiss, and once he closes the door behind me, I feel a smoldering heat behind me.

Jory's chest molds against my back as I'm kissing Breckon and I feel like the cream center of the most delicious cookie ever.

I'm already heated up and ready to go from Caleb's sensual assault on my lips earlier, and I know I'm about to face something I've never experienced before. As Breckon continues to kiss me, I shudder as Jory's mouth sucks on the back of my neck. There are hands on my waist, and they glide up under my shirt to span over my tummy. Suddenly, hot fingers find one of my nipples and begin to twist. I can't breathe.

Breck's mouth slides over my cheek to my ear. "We're so glad you're here, baby. We've been waiting for this."

"Yes, we have, beautiful." Jory's voice in my other ear.

They simultaneously begin to lick and suck each of my ears while both nipples are now being stimulated. My panties are already soaked, and I don't know how I'm going to handle this erotic assault.

Jory picks me up and carries me to the bed while Breck follows. It doesn't take me long to notice that they've pushed both their full-sized beds together into the center of the room to create one enormous sleeping space. Or not sleeping, in this case. As I lay back on the cool sheet that has been lain across both mattresses, my arms are thrust over my head and two strong, warm hands hold them there. Breckon runs kisses down my chin, throat, and chest while Jory holds my hands in place with one strong fist. His other fist is stroking himself outside his boxer briefs, and I wonder why he hasn't removed them yet.

"You want this?" he whispers, looking down at his engorged dick and then back at me with a smile.

I nod and am about to reply when my panties are being slid down my legs and then tossed to the ground. Breckon slides his tongue along my slit in one, long lick, and then lifts his head up, a questioning look in his eyes. "Why does your pussy smell like watermelon?"

I bite back a grin and say, "I'll tell you later. Just eat it like it's a real watermelon."

He chuckles and bends down, licking inside my hole as I groan in pleasure. When his tongue slides up my clit, I whimper and almost come.

Jory lets go of my hands and leans down to give each of my breasts equal attention. My too-sensitive nipples stand at attention.

Breckon slides two fingers inside me and begins to pump them in and out as he continues to bestow attention on my lips and clit. I gasp when one of his wet fingers finds my other hole and he pushes it in slowly. With what he's doing down there, combined with what Jory's doing on my nipples, I going to come hard—and quick.

Jory lifts his head and looks down at me with his intense yellowish-green eyes. His fingers find my nipple while his mouth captures my lips. He begins a slow, sensuous kiss at the same time Breck inserts his fangs into one of my lady lips. He begins to suck as his fingers continue their work on my clit and ass. At the first pull of blood from my labia, an orgasm as strong as a tsunami roars through me and I scream into Jory's mouth.

It was all so much at once. My mouth, my breast, my clit, my tight hole... I am on the verge of passing out from sensory overload.

Jory's mouth continues to plunder mine as I scream and moan into it. I'm not even down from my high when I feel a thick entrance prodding my soaked core. Breckon pushes his way in.

My eyes roll back in my head at the sensation of him filling me all the way up. My hips move in time with his and then Jory climbs off the bed.

Breckon lifts me up so we're sitting face to face, his cock lodged deep inside me, and he tells Jory, "My turn to kiss this beautiful woman."

His mouth and tongue find mine as his arms wrap around my shoulders. We continue to move together, and I still haven't caught my breath. The flesh between my legs is on fire and ready to explode again. I glance to my right to see Jory standing there, his cock out and his hand gliding up and down it as he watches us. His eyes are bright yellow and smoldering with desire.

Breckon slams me down on the bed and pushes my knees apart to fuck me hard and fast. He thrusts in and out of me at a punishing pace and the sight is more than I can handle. Jory suddenly hops on the bed, straddles my chest, and grabs my hair. He slowly puts his cock in my mouth and begins to slowly pump in and out of me. He groans loudly when I take him all the way into my throat, my other hand sliding up and down the base with the moisture from my mouth.

"Fuck..." he whispers, tossing his head back and closing his eyes.

Suddenly, Jory hisses out as if he's in pain, but then quickly relaxes. I look up to see Breckon's face behind Jory's shoulder, and the blood on his lips tells me he's bitten Jory as he fucks me hard. The sight is too erotic for me to handle, and I scream around Jory's cock as another orgasm thunders through me. My pussy milks Breck's cock as he suddenly stills inside me with a loud groan. I didn't even have enough time to register that, as Jory's dick explodes into my mouth, his cum sliding down my throat as I swallow all of it. Jory grunts out his release, shuddering as the last drops fall onto my tongue.

Both guys collapse on either side of me, all of us panting so hard I'm sure the mirror in the bathroom is probably fogged up from all this heat.

Once I find my breath, I turn to look at Breck, who is running featherlight touches up and down my stomach, sides, and to my thigh. "Did you bite Jory?"

"Sure did," he says, leaning down to kiss my nose.

"It was awesome," Jory adds, running his hand down my stomach, causing me to shudder.

"Dragon blood is spicy. It's kind of an extra rush," Breckon adds.

"What does mine taste like?" I ask.

Breck grins. "Watermelon."

I slap him. "Liar."

"I'm kidding. But seriously, what's up with that?"

Staring at them both sheepishly, I explain the Kool-Aid trick.

"Very clever, little witch," Breckon replies with a smile before leaning down to kiss me.

Since spring is almost here, we've been moved to outdoor sports for gym class. This semester: soccer. I loathe the sport and wish for more badminton. But as I glance at the obstacle course, I'm grateful it's not *that*.

I look up at the blue sky, which is crowded with bloated clouds, and then close my eyes as the sun and a light breeze touch my skin. I think again about a weekend pass. My first year will be up at the end of the summer and I should have one waiting on me by the end of July, just in time for my birthday. I begin to daydream about where I'll go. I mean, of course I'll go home, if I can, but if we have to stick to someplace local—like, Montana local—I'll go on the internet and see what's around here. If I have to camp out at the mall or an all-you-can-eat buffet all weekend, so be it. Anyplace but here would do.

A few weeks ago, I heard Jory and Breckon talk about just camping out in the woods for their weekend pass. That didn't sound very fun to me, but if they like that shit, then more power to them. I can barely handle glamping, let alone actual sleeping on the ground, no electricity, eating MREs or freshly caught whatever. I shudder slightly at the thought of having to barbeque a snake or something for nourishment.

Then I thought about Jory. And Breckon. And both of them together. Then, another kind of delicious shudder began to ripple through me...

Cough. "Whore." *Cough.*

I whip my head around as I'm standing on the field, waiting for the ball to be lurched my way. I see Eliza standing there, arms folded across her chest, staring smugly at me.

I narrow my eyes at her. "Excuse me?"

"The fact that you turned around tells me you are one."

I snort and smirk. "At least I'm getting some." Why deny it at this point?

"It's bad enough you took the two hottest jocks. You had to take the new hottie, too?"

How the fuck did she know about me and Caleb? Was she spying on us on the bleachers?

"He's not your type, trust me." I whip my head around to

make sure I won't be hit by an incoming soccer ball, then turn back around. "But if you wanna take a crack at him, go for it." I shrug as if I don't care.

I plan to later get with Caleb and let him know that Eliza has a raging case of herpes. Might throw in some crabs, too, for good measure.

She lifts her chin and smiles. "I think I will."

It's amazing how fast I shut her down. Had I pitched a fit about being called a whore—which did piss me off, by the way—it would have fueled her fire, and she would have won. Still, I felt kind of like I broke weak letting her call me that, but by the look on her face, it didn't give her as much satisfaction as an irate reaction from me would have.

Huh, ya learn something new every day.

"Heads up!" I hear someone yell, and I immediately duck.

Unfortunately for her, the ball goes sailing past my head and clocks Eliza right in the boob.

She wails, grabs her chest, and falls to the grassy field below. "Ow. I need to see the nurse."

I stare hard at her as people rush over. She cracks open an eye and looks at me, and she seems amused and triumphant. *Okay, well played, Eliza, well played.*

At least I'd taught her something. Even if it was the work of a deviant.

It's not like we're all angels here, anyway. Well, except the nurse.

"Say hi to Karissa for me!" I wave as two of her minions help her off the field.

Chapter 11

I swallow the bite of brussels sprouts and grin while I pick up my milk glass. "You got a thing for redheads?"

Caleb turns to glance at Eliza once more, who's smiling coyly at him, and then back to me. "Girl, I don't discriminate on hair color. But, succubuses? Uh, hellz no. Won't touch one with a ten-foot pole."

Oh, good. I won't have to lie about the herpes and crabs now.

"I don't think the plural—"

"Well, she wants you bad. I bet she's freaky in bed," I interrupt Astrid to egg him on.

"They are."

I turn to look at Breckon, who's not eating, but watching our interaction closely. We all just sit at the same cafeteria table now. Why hide anything?

"Spill it, man," Caleb says to Breck, mischief glittering in his gaze.

The vampire briefly looks at me, then back to Caleb. "Nah, I don't kiss and tell and all that."

"You fu... screw her?" I ask incredulously, jerking my head in Eliza's direction.

Breckon chuckles. "Wouldn't you like to know?"

Jory elbows him in the ribs and then stabs a piece of salmon with his fork. "Quit."

Breckon just grins.

"Wow," Astrid takes the word right out of my mouth.

I glance at Alicia, who's watching the interaction with rapt interest, but of course keeping her mouth shut. I should be more like Alicia. Maybe she can teach me how she does that. I snort at my own idea.

"We're not having that discussion here," Breckon says. "Especially with the number of ears in this room."

I wave a hand. "Eliza's always ear-hustling. I don't think she can hear us from this far, though."

"Later, baby." Breckon winks at me.

Caleb watches the interaction and fans himself. "Damn."

The inevitable horn strikes the air. "Caleb Owens, one point has been deducted from your account."

We all laugh.

"I frickin' hate that robot bi…wench!" he snaps.

"Welcome to Larchwood." Astrid giggles as she moves her rice around on her plate.

The clinking of glasses and silverware can be heard for a few quiet moments as we eat until I get up the nerve to ask Caleb, "What did you do to get here, anyway?"

I meant to ask it in private, but it seems we are probably gonna have our mouths occupied whenever we're alone.

At his hesitation, I jump in with, "Uh, I don't mean to put you on the spot. You don't have to answer."

Caleb shakes his head and grins. "Nah, it's fine. I don't have anything to hide. I don't even think I should be here, honestly. But it is what it is."

"I think a lot of us feel that way," Alicia says quietly.

"We'll get your story next, *mamacita*," Caleb says to her with a wink and a megawatt smile.

Alicia's cheeks immediately flame pink. She slides some hair behind her ear and then shoves a brussels sprout into her mouth. The whole thing. I bite back a laugh. She's so dang cute.

"So, quick background. I'm from Dallas. Born and raised—mostly by my mom, Dad wasn't around much. I didn't grow up with any abuse or nothin' like that. Just was kinda left on my own a lot. Mom's a witch, taught me a few things, but I don't think anyone knew the extent of my powers. I still don't know if my dad's a warlock or not. Once I came into my powers, I wasn't able to get in touch with him. Mom says she doesn't know, but I think—how the he...ck do you not know if your baby daddy's a witch or warlock? Anyway, I suspect he is, due to my undiluted power."

Wow. Ether this dude is mega-powerful, or a megalomaniac with an inflated sense of self. Guess I'll find out soon.

"Undiluted power?" Jory asks as he tosses his napkin onto his very empty plate.

Caleb chuckles. "Yeah, they actually locked me in segregation when I first got here. Said my powers had to be checked before I could be around other supes."

I sit up straighter in my chair. "Segregation? What?"

The young warlock looks at all of us, confusion coloring his face. "You guys don't know that there are literally cells down below here?" He points to the floor. "Like a fu...freaking dungeon."

We all look at each other. "No way," I breathe.

"Yes, way, spicy witch. I mean, it's not exactly like a dungeon, but definitely like jail."

"A jail within a prison, how fitting," I comment dryly.

Caleb clicks his tongue and winks at me. "Exactly. I was only down there a couple days. Promised them I wouldn't do magic without supervision and all that. And I see they take that sh...stuff very seriously here." His eyes flick to the final five rules posted above the double-doorway that leads out of the cafeteria.

"So, anyway. My first infraction was just B.S. I was in high school at the time. Dude was bullying me and sh...crap for being gay."

Honk! "Caleb Owens, one point has been deducted from your account."

I look around the lunchroom to see it's mostly empty now. Just our group is left, along with some staff cleaning off the tables.

"W-T-F. I didn't say any bad words."

"You can't say C-R-A-P." I spell it out like I'm in third grade.

"Wow." Caleb shakes his head. "Anyway, he and I were on the basketball team. So one day during practice—you know, because the guy wouldn't bully me in public, just in the locker rooms—I made sure his fingers got caught in the net when he went for a slam dunk. He broke all the fingers on his left hand. He was out for the rest of the season."

"Serves him right, I say," Astrid chimes in. "I hate bullies."

"You kids done?" an older woman wearing the cafeteria workers' uniform asks.

We nod and she and another worker whisk our plates and cups away.

"Yeah, but somehow, someone could tell it wasn't just an accident. Dude was hanging there for a few minutes—by his fingers, screaming—until they could get a ladder and help him down. I may or may not have been smiling at him the whole time while the rest of the team was scrambling to help."

"Did he bother you again?" Jory asks.

"Oh, he...ck no. Wouldn't even look my way. It was like he knew."

"What else?" I ask, my head resting on my hand, elbow on the table. I glance to my right to see Jory and Breckon both staring at me instead of Caleb. I bet they're thinking about last night too.

"I did okay after that. I was warned by the supernatural cops—who showed up at my mom's place the next day. Had no idea they existed. So I graduated, and then walked the line for a bit after that, until I absolutely had to use my magic.

"After a couple semesters, I realized college wasn't for me, so I worked a few odd jobs, waiting tables and stuff, while I tried to get in with this acting troupe in Dallas. I kept auditioning but they kept turning me down. Then my dream play came up—*Hamilton*. I just had to nail the part. I put a sickness spell on the other guy auditioning for the part of Marquis de Lafayette so I could get it." He shrugs. "We were the only two black dudes in the running.

"Well, obviously I got the part, and right after, another visit from the cops. Telling me I had two strikes. I mean, how the fudge did these cops know I was using magic to begin with, and the guy just didn't have a stomach bug?"

Astrid shakes her head. "Trust me, they know. Honestly, I think they have a witch in their back pocket. One who tracks magic. That includes the magic that emits from shifters, vampires, and everything else." She waves a hand in Jory and Breck's direction.

"Huh. Good to know. Thanks, Astrid." Caleb winks at her.

He needs to stop doing that. It's making me weirdly jealous. As if I have any monogamous ground to stand on.

"Third was the worst of them all. I had proudly served two years in that troupe, taking *Hamilton* all over the country. I was aiming for Broadway, and after that, Hollywood, when I found myself with a bit of a problem." He blows out a breath. "The guy I'd been seeing got arrested. He was one of the secondary characters in the show, so we were always together. Yeah, we had smoked a little weed, done some coke from time to time. Nothing outrageous." He shrugs. "But the feds had picked him up on drug trafficking. Guess he'd been a serious dealer before he went into the show. I found out later he joined the troupe to get away from those people and that environment."

"And probably the cops," Breck said wryly from his seat.

Caleb nods. "Yeah, that, too. I had a dream the night before about his sentencing hearing. They were gonna give him twenty years. I thought that was outrageous. My first thought was to put a spell on the judge to get him off, but then I thought about my two prior infractions. They would know if I did magic. I had the whole night to think about it, as Sean was getting sentenced the next day. After careful thought, I decided I was gonna do it. Whatever punishment they gave me couldn't be worse than twenty years in federal prison. For a gay man, at that. So instead, here I am. Two years instead of twenty. Seems worth it, right?"

"Yeah, but only if he's gonna wait for you," I said.

Caleb chuckled, but the glint from his eye was gone. "Nah, judge gave him five years' probation, no jailtime. Thought things were working out—we could be together. But he promptly dumped me as soon as the supernatural cops picked me up. See, Sean doesn't know I'm a warlock. Just thought the judge was in a good mood that day. So, no need to thank me. He didn't even ask what *I* was being picked up for. Just never talked to me again."

"Ass…hat," I grumble.

Jory whistles low between his teeth. "Harsh."

Caleb scoffs. "You can say that again. I've killed him fifty different violent ways in my head. Of course, that's where it'll stay. No more magic for me."

"But you're psychic, aren't you?" I ask.

He shrugs. "Yeah, I guess."

"So you didn't know Sean wasn't going to dump you?" Jory asks.

Caleb sighs. "It doesn't work that way."

"How does it work?" I ask.

"It's time for you kids to vacate the cafeteria."

We look up to see Headmaster Griggs standing there with his hands in the pockets of his dress slacks. His jaw tics as he stares at me for a few long extra seconds and then the rest of the group. "Staff need to finish cleaning for the morning meal, then go rest for the night."

We all get up and head toward the exits. They've already cleared off our table, so what is left for them to do? Wipe it off, push in the chairs, and shut the lights off?

Griggs mutters his thanks and then leaves the lunchroom with all of us following behind.

Chapter 12

Caleb fans himself. "Between you, that shifter, the vampire, and that hot A.F. *mamacita* Alicia—not to mention that headmaster—I think I might just spontaneously combust!" He says this in a high-pitched Southern drawl like he's some damsel from a western movie.

I chuckle as we again sit on the bleachers, watching the swimmers. Astrid and Alicia are again in their dorms and I wonder why they think they need to study so much. We were forced to come here. This isn't college, and we were promised a high school diploma. Or was it a GED? Either way, study, schmudy.

"What's up with that headmaster, anyway? Why's someone so young and smokin' running this joint?" he asks as he grabs my hand and laces his fingers through mine.

"I have asked myself the same question for the past several months." I chuckle. "And you want in on a secret?"

"Duh."

"I think he wants me." I mean, I know he wants me after that whole finger-banging incident in my dorm.

"Wow, really? How do you keep up, my friend?" he asks as he lifts my hand to his lips and kisses my knuckles.

A whistle blows and we look toward the pool to see all the swimmers dive in and begin swimming furiously to the other side to get there first. The competition is a turn-on, not to mention all the muscular, writhing bodies splashing toward the finish line.

Caleb gives a sound of approval as he watches them.

I chuckle. "My thoughts exactly."

He turns to me and puts his hand on my jaw as he stares into my eyes. "They're hot, but you're hotter."

Grinning, I say, "I know."

He leans down like he's going to kiss me, but instead, he nips my bottom lip with his teeth. "No kisses for you."

I pout like before and he just grins. "That doesn't work on me."

Laughing, our hands still linked, I rest my head on his shoulder. "Tell me, how much psychic power do you have?"

"I honestly don't know. I get dreams—premonitions—but that seems to be it. I can't do palm readings or any of that other shit." He slaps his hand over his mouth.

I lift my head from his shoulder and grin. "Robo-bitch can't seem to hear us out here. Inside buildings and for some reason near the obstacle course, but not out here. Or in our dorm rooms."

"Oh, thank fuck," he replies.

I chuckle at his response.

"Why do you ask?"

"I need to solve a murder," I say flatly.

"Oh, okay, so nothing major then," he deadpans in reply.

I laugh again. I love this guy.

"Tell me about the murder," he says quietly after a few more minutes of silence. We've been watching the swim team practice their laps and I smiled quite a few times when Breckon had beat them to the other side of the pool, even if by mere seconds.

"A filthy vamp killed my grandma and I need to find out where he's at."

"How filthy vuz he?" he asks in a Dracula voice while waggling his eyebrows.

I shake with laughter then slap his chest. "Stop! This is serious."

"Okay, sorry. Tell me about this grimy Nosferatu."

"I…" Pausing, I'm not sure where to start. All I have are childhood memories manifested into nightmares, and what my mother told me. "I don't know." I end on a sigh.

"You have to know something. You know a vamp killed your grandma. How do you know that?"

"My mom told me," I reply.

"And she doesn't know where this bloodsucker is?" Caleb asks, running his hand down my leg.

Now, I wore my gym shorts and hoodie only, so I'm glad I shaved yesterday, because his touch is pretty magical.

"I don't think so, but I think she knows who he is."

"And she won't tell you because…?"

I blow out a breath between my lips. "She says she's trying to protect me."

"From?" He lets the question hang in the air.

"The dude. The vampire."

Caleb looks out across the pool. "He's that dangerous, huh?"

"So she says."

"And she doesn't think you can handle him?"

I shake my head against his shoulder. "No. Or she doesn't even want me to try."

"Parents are pretty overprotective that way. Not necessarily a bad thing."

I'm growing frustrated. "I know, but this fucking vamp killed my gram. I'm not gonna sit by and just let him get away with it."

"Understandable. But how do you know your mom isn't doing something about it herself? She too is a witch... right?"

I lift my head from his shoulder, unlink my fingers with his, and narrow my eyes. "You like to play devil's advocate, don't you?"

Caleb stares down at me smugly. "Sometimes."

I stand, now getting mad. "I don't understand why I can't get a straight fucking answer from you."

"Is there a problem here?"

I turn to see Breckon standing there, Jory quickly walking to catch up.

"No, no problem," I grit out, storming down the bleachers and to the ground to get away.

I don't know why I'm so angry. I don't know why I got my hopes up that Caleb could help me find my grandma's killer. Guess I was expecting too much out of the aloof, carefree, *psychic* warlock.

Shame on me.

I storm off toward the dorms, but before I reach the door that brings me inside, a strong hand lands on my shoulder and spins me around. I look up into Breckon's nearly black eyes. "You shouldn't go to bed angry."

"Who says I'm going to bed?"

He glances over my shoulder to the dorm building, then back to me. "Foolish assumption."

I stare up into his eyes until he leans down and kisses me softly. He presses his forehead against mine and whispers, "We all care about you, Paige. It's a complicated situation."

"*What's* a complicated situation?" I ask, hating the way my voice goes up in an octave in frustration.

"You. Me. Jory. Caleb." He blows out a breath and looks

away, but his touch is still igniting a fire inside of me. "Even Griggs."

I blink once. Twice. By the third, I feel my blinks are dramatic enough to show that I'm demanding an answer. One that never comes. "You're telling me that all four of you want me." I exhale hard. "While, yeah, I guess I get that—not that I see what any of you see in me—what I don't understand is why you all are okay with it. Don't even one of you want me for yourself?"

Breckon's hands find my cheeks as he stares into my eyes. "God, Paige, yes. I wish I could have you all to myself. To lock you in my room. Tie you to my bed and never let you go. Just you and me alone. Truth is, we all want you for ourselves. But it's not what's meant to be. There has to be three. There just has to be."

His lips are millimeters from mine, and I want to devour them so badly, but know I can't because I need answers. "You keep saying that, but you never explain. You say three, but now I see four."

I'm glad the night isn't very cold, because he leads me by the hand to the bench that sits outside the main entrance to the dorm room.

He indicates for me to sit, then takes the empty space next to me. "Paige, there are bigger things at work here. We promise we'll explain them to you eventually, but until the three of us are all on the same page, we can't. Just know that you're very, very special. We knew it from the moment we laid eyes on you."

I begin to protest at his cryptic comments, but he silences me with a kiss. My body responds to him immediately, and before I know it, I'm straddling his lap while I rake my fingers through his thick, damp hair. His wandering hands grip the nape of my neck to push me closer to his mouth before the other is snaking down my back and then around to my stomach. He splays his hand over the bare flesh there and gently rubs circles with his thumb. I shudder at the feeling of his hands and mouth on me.

He stands without breaking our kiss and picks me up, my legs wrapping around his waist. He carries me into the dorms and seems to know his way, as he heads straight to my room and opens the door with the hand holding my right ass cheek. Turning around and using his back, he pushes the door open, and I turn and look, relieved to see Astrid isn't there. She must be with Axel.

Without words, he puts his mouth back on mine, our tongues dueling and twisting erotically with each other before he lays me down on the bed. Breckon has me stripped bare in mere seconds before he's peeling off his track pants and zip-up sweatshirt, throwing them to the floor. When he lies down on top of me, his hard chest causes my nipples to pebble under him. His hand slides down my belly and finds my warm, wet core, and I groan and shudder at the feel of his fingers slowly gliding over my most sensitive spot. Reaching down, I stroke his hard, silky smooth cock and take it into my hands. He hisses against my lips and I continue to stroke until I have to stop, because my body is shuddering and my mouth is whimpering with its first climax of the night.

Before I'm even down off my high, I gently guide him into my soaking wet heat, panting when he's fully seated inside me. Breckon pushes up on his arms and stares down at me. "Fuck, you're so damn beautiful, Paige. I really do want you all to myself."

Before I can respond, he leans down and takes one nipple into his mouth and sucks hard, which causes my body to clamp around his cock. He groans against my breast as he begins to pump in and out of me.

I relish the feeling of his relentless pace when he lets go of my nipple with a sucking pop. He then leans back and grabs both my hipbones in his iron grip and continues to slam in and out of me, watching the action with hooded eyes and parted lips.

The friction is delicious and consuming, and as he lazily looks up into my eyes as he fucks me, I can't help but feel a deep, permanent connection with Breckon. His eyes are fiery and dark, but not soulless. I can see the desire, passion, and care there. His look takes me over the edge, and I grip Breckon's shoulders, digging my fingers in when I feel myself tipping over the abyss, losing myself to another mind-numbing orgasm that he shares with me. He stills his movements as he loses himself to his desire.

God, I really hope they're right when they say vamps can't impregnate a witch.

He leans down and kisses me softly. "That was amazing. You're amazing," he says against my lips.

I can only sigh my response with a smile against his.

Chapter 13

Breckon must have snuck out sometime after we fell asleep together because he was gone by morning. Astrid told me she hadn't seen him when she came in around three a.m.

"How do you keep up with them all? I barely have enough emotional energy for one," Astrid mumbles as we head to the Practical Magic building.

I don't have an answer for her because I don't even know it myself, so I just stay quiet. I'm admittedly feeling confused by all the boys in my life and am trying to sort everything out mentally. Also a little embarrassed that I haven't even once attempted to play hard to get.

I'm way too easy.

We reach the building and wander inside to see most everyone is there, seated on the floor in a circle. I indicate for Caleb and Rainlily to make a space so Astrid and I can squeeze in. I purposely sit next to Caleb.

There's a low chatter to the room so I lean in close. "I'm sorry."

He grins at me. "For what?"

I narrow my eyes at him. "You know what. I just don't do well with vague explanations and getting the runaround."

"Was I giving you the runaround?" he asks.

"Not really," I say quietly. "I just need someone who's on my side. Not my mom's. She gives me the runaround all the time. I don't need it from my friends, too."

"I was just asking questions, silly witch."

I sigh long and dramatically. "I know, I know. I'm just… I don't know. I think I just want to hit the easy button on this one. Have someone tell me where this POS is so I can go hunt him down myself."

"You think you can take down a vampire by yourself?" Caleb asks, quirking an eyebrow at me.

"No, I don't. Not without—"

"…Magic," Headmaster Griggs, seemingly finishing his welcoming of us to his class.

Caleb shoots me a look. "In the words of Confucius, 'Those who seek revenge should dig two graves'."

"Then I'll bring a dagger *and* a shovel," I reply dryly.

Caleb snorts but straightens up when the headmaster asks the class for an answer. To a question we apparently missed.

Oh, God, please don't call on me.

"Astrid?"

"Both. Runes can be used for good and bad."

Whew. Thank the Lord he picked the runes girl.

"Correct." Headmaster walks over to a display easel I hadn't seen the first time we were in this building and begins to draw symbols—runes—on the butcher paper held there by a large clip. I don't recognize any of the runes. Not that I've seen many in my life.

"Do you ever use these?" I ask Caleb, pointing to the page Griggs draws on.

He lifts a shoulder and lets it fall before popping a piece of gum in his mouth. He offers me a piece, but I decline. "I have a couple times, but to try to master, it's hard. They're a total bi…beast to memorize."

Great, as if I needed something else clouding up my already crowded brain.

"I'm going to just give you the answers right now. Write these down—draw them and put its use next to each symbol."

My lazy ass pulls out my phone, zooms in on the paper while Master's back is turned, and snaps a picture. I didn't feel like pulling out my notebook. I quickly stash the phone under my butt as he turns around.

He eyes me for a brief second, seeing that I'm not writing it down, but doesn't say anything. I'm sure he's looking forward to failing me so we can have a little "one-on-one" tutoring. Not that I would mind.

"Healing rune," he starts. "Where do we apply it?"

Miss Goody-Goody raises her hand.

"Yes, Astrid?" He points at her.

"Anywhere near the wound. Arm wound, anywhere on the arm. Stomach wound, anywhere on the stomach. Back wound, anywhere on the back. And so on."

"Right again, young lady." Griggs smiles at Astrid and I frown. I wish he'd drop the young man, young lady thing. He talks like he's eighty.

I have a thought, so I raise my hand.

"Yes, Paige?"

"What if you're suffering from like an internal thing? Stomach pain, joint pain, stuff like that?"

"Same concept, just draw the rune on the skin near the pain source."

"It just makes the pain stop? Heals the wound?" Caleb asks.

Headmaster nods. "Yes. And no. Runes work better on supes than on humans. Nobody really knows why, but some suspect it's because supes believe they can work, and humans do not."

"So there's an element of belief and trust involved for it to work," Rainlily says more than asks.

"Exactly," Griggs says.

He flips the page with the healing runes over, and begins to draw others, with their descriptions next to them, on a fresh piece of paper.

"Write these down as well," he commands.

I go to take a picture again but get caught this time. My face flushes and I stow the phone back under my ass.

"Paige, you'll never learn to draw them if you don't actually draw them."

I was already unzipping my messenger bag and pulling out my notebook and a pencil. "I know, I'm sorry."

Sorry I got caught. I have every intention of drawing them eventually—the subject fascinates me. I just wanted to have them permanently captured in case I ever need one in a quick pinch. Guess I can take a picture of my paper after I draw it.

I quickly scribble out what Griggs has on the paper.

"As the class goes on, the runes we learn are going to become more powerful. These ones, as with the rest, are to only be used with great caution, and usually in emergencies only."

There are five runes of different shapes and sizes, and are labeled: Strength, Speed, Sight, Hearing, and Power-Up.

"Unlike the healing runes, these can be drawn anywhere on the body, and are usually just used for yourself. For instance, let's say you're being chased by a very vicious dog and need to get away. If you draw the speed rune on, say, your forearm, this will cause you to run at great speeds."

"Like Flash," a warlock in the circle says. I notice the kids closest to the easel had all turned around, their backs to us in the back of the circle, and were facing front.

Griggs chuckles. "Yeah, kinda. Not as fast as Flash, though. Just enough speed to outrun whatever's chasing you."

"What's the sight one for?" I ask.

"Good question, Paige. Perhaps said dog is chasing you at night. It's very dark. No streetlamps, no full moon. You could draw the sight rune on your arm as well, help you see in the dark."

"Like… like… well, a dog?"

He laughs again. "Yes, like a dog. Gotta be a match for your opponent."

"Doesn't sound like the dog is an opponent in this story. He's a terrorist." Caleb laughs.

I clear my throat. "How am I gonna draw a rune if it's so dark I need help seeing?"

"Good question," Griggs responds. "This is why we're going to teach you to draw without looking."

"I don't have a Stile," Rainlily says, and I'm impressed she knows what it's called, as I had been clueless when I first saw Astrid's.

"I know," the headmaster says. "Rainlily, please go to that cabinet over there and pull out the wooden box."

She nods and heads across the room as we watch. She opens the door to the closet and plucks a large wooden box. She nearly drops it, it's so heavy.

Griggs gets to her so fast, I could swear he's a vampire. When he stops, I can see the shirt sleeve of his left arm is up and a rune is drawn there. I look to the easel to see "Speed" next to the symbol he's got on his arm. He produces a Stile from his pocket and quickly draws a different rune on Rainlily's arm. Instantly, she's holding the box as if it were no heavier than a small pillow.

"Whoa," she breathes, spinning the box around on her palm.

"Please pass out the Stiles to the students," he says to the hippie witch.

She grins and does as she's asked, happily handing one Stile to each student. But by the time she reaches the last few, the box is getting heavy for her, and she can barely carry it back to the closet. It's like she holds a brick now, not a pillow—and it's empty.

"Wow, that wore off fast," I comment to no one and everyone.

"Yes, it did," Griggs replies. "I did that on purpose."

I turn the Stile around in my hands. It looks different than Astrid's. Hers looks more antique and heirloom-looking. This just looks like an oversized letter opener. It does have the school's crest on the handle, though.

"Everyone, find a partner, we're going to experiment."

I partner up with Caleb, and Astrid and Alicia face each other.

"Does it hurt?" I hear Alicia ask quietly.

"Not really," Astrid whispers back.

"Okay. Everyone facing the door, set your Stile down on the mat. Everyone facing the east wall, look at the easel and choose a rune to draw on your partner."

I'm facing the door, so I drop mine to the mat, and see Caleb has his Stile out. He looks nervous. I smile reassuringly at him. "Don't be afraid. I'll be fine. I'm excited."

"I've never drawn one on anyone else before. Heck, I've only drawn a couple on myself." He looks at the easel, and I look, too. Then, I look down as he puts the Stile to my forearm, but then hesitates. "How big is it supposed to be?"

I burst out a laugh and try to cover it with a cough. Astrid giggles behind me.

Griggs ignores us and says, "About the size of a quarter."

Caleb licks his lips. He holds the knife like a pen and begins to carve into my forearm. It burns for a split second and I can hear gasps and hisses around the room of those getting marked along with me. The pain recedes quickly, and amazingly, a half-moon symbol with two dots on the top and bottom of it appear as if he'd drawn it with a Sharpie.

"Cool," I say, smiling at him.

I turn around and students are zipping all over the place. Guess we all had the same idea. I run to the door and back in less than two seconds flat to see Alicia standing with her hands over her ears. The super-hearing rune isn't agreeing with her.

"Okay, students, now reverse and repeat. R and R."

"Ow," Alicia says, her hands over her ears. "Is he shouting?" She juts her chin at the instructor. I just shake my head no with a laugh.

Caleb stashes his Stile and I pick mine up from the mat. I decide to draw the strength rune on him. It's a bit weird drawing with a knife, but I find a comfortable position to hold it in and then draw a vertical rectangle with a squiggly line down the middle. The Stile lights up for a brief second, making my hand warm, and then it's done. I guess I didn't notice that happen to Caleb or the headmaster when they drew their runes. It felt like the Stile was pulling magic from me. I drop the knife and stand with my hand on my hips. "Lift me up."

Caleb grins and rubs his hands together before I leap into his arms. He's got me in a fireman's hold before he lifts me up over his head like a barbell and begins bench-pressing me up and down a few times. I'm giggling, but then I hear, "Oh, cra...ckle."

I feel myself falling and scream. Strong arms catch me before I fall to the floor. I look up to see Griggs holding me. Our blue eyes lock eyes before he sets me down.

He looks at Caleb. "These are sixty-second runes. You have to be very cognizant of when they'll wear off."

"Thanks for the save, Master," I say to his retreating figure.

He ignores me, walking to the closet to retrieve the box, and then goes around the room, collecting the Stiles.

"How are we supposed to practice if we can't take them back to our rooms?" Astrid asks, dropping hers into the box.

I bite back a smile. She's just being a smartass now. I throw her a look and she winks at me.

"You don't. Practice is only done here, under an instructor's supervision. Under *my* supervision. Rule number five." He points to the rules on the wall above the doors. The class groans.

Where hasn't he posted those damn rules? I resist an eye roll.

"You, may, however, draw them on paper. In fact, I encourage it. Get to know how to draw them fast. Try them in different sizes. We'll learn how each size affects the runes' lasting power."

He goes on about size, stamina, and lasting power and I have to get my mind out of the gutter for the rest of the class.

Chapter 14

"How's your tit?" I ask Eliza as we're putting on our soccer cleats.

"Perfect," she says as she ties hers. "Both of them."

Does she think I actually care? I was trying to mimic her smartass question about me having mud in my vag from earlier in the year after I completely fumbled the obstacle course. Maybe she's using my own tactic on me.

She continues, "They were perfect before and they're still perfect. Perky, full, and ready for action."

I make a gagging noise. "Well, that was a visual I didn't need and now won't be able to get out of my head." I get up and head to the field as I hear her cackling behind me.

I'm gonna turn her into a toad.

We play boys against the girls and I really can't understand why the coaches think this is okay. The boys outmatch us in every physical way—add to the fact they're supes to boot, and it's just not fair.

But wait. I can outsmart them. Distract them.

"Girls, huddle up," I say when the coach blows the whistle at a foul. I'm not the captain, but I just put myself in charge.

"We're getting creamed," I say. "They're stronger than us, but we're smarter, right?"

"Yeah!" the girls yell out.

I look at Eliza. "Hey, magic tits—I'm gonna need you to whip one out as soon as one of the guys goes to kick the ball."

She stares at me in horror and looks around the huddle. "Paige, no. I'm not doing that."

I cock my head to the side. "But I thought you said they were perfect and ready for action?" I frown. "Wait—unless you meant breastfeeding?"

The girls burst out laughing. Eliza's eyes burn into me angrily, but instead of lashing out, she puts on a cool countenance. "Not yet. Gotta wait for Breck or Jory to put a baby in me first."

Everyone laughs again. I can tell she's trying to make me jealous, but it's not working. I just laugh as well. I get that Breckon could technically get her pregnant since they're both vampires, but it's not gonna happen. That reminds me, I never did get a straight answer out of him whether or not he's ever fucked her...

A whistle blows and we clap collectively before returning to the field.

"Some cleavage? Something? Come on," I say quietly to Eliza as she stands next to me near the goalie.

"Why don't you ask one of your witch friends?" She juts her chin and Alicia and Astrid, who are talking and not paying attention at all.

I raise my eyebrows at her, as we both can see that A and A are both, well, AA sized. Eliza's boobs are bigger than mine, but mine aren't all that bad. "How about on the count of three, we both flash? It doesn't even have to be boobs, just bra. That might throw off Jory's kick." I look at the redheaded dragon, who's steeling himself with a serious expression, breathing in and out, ready to launch the soccer ball.

"We won't lose any points for doing that?" she asks.

"What 'final five' rule are we breaking?" I put up air quotes.

She shrugs. "None, I guess."

I don't need Jory seeing her tits, anyway. He swings his leg back to kick.

"One. Two. Three!"

I whistle and Jory looks up as I lift my shirt.

Eliza doesn't.

Jory misses the kick.

Eliza bursts out laughing.

Mr. Johnson blows his whistle and tells me to warm the bench. Then calls in Rainlily to take my place. He narrows his eyes at me. "You report to the headmaster's office after gym class is over."

"Right-o," I say. Then I look at Eliza, who's smiling smugly at me. I shake a finger at her. "Fool me once, bitch," I mouth at her.

She flips me off.

Oh, well. I thought we were getting somewhere. Guess the redheaded tart really wants to stay on my bad side.

"What am I gonna do with you, Paige?" Griggs asks as I'm seated on his couch in his office.

"What do you *want* to do with me?" I ask, suggestively bouncing my eyebrows at him.

"Stop it. Enough with the flirtation. I have a job to do and you're making it very difficult."

I stand up and point toward the closed door. "You freakin' started it! Yeah, I think you're hot, but in no way did I invite you into my room that night to do… to do… you know, what you did! You could have at least stayed and let me finish you off!"

He purses his lips and looks down at his glass desktop. He

taps the pen he's holding and lets out a deep breath. He points at the chair. "Real talk, right now. Sit down and I'm gonna shoot straight with you. This stays between us, and if you *ever* repeat any of this, I'll call you a liar. Get it?"

I nod.

"Say you understand, Paige." His jaw bunches in annoyance.

"Yes, I understand. Yes, this will stay between us."

Griggs measures me with a hard stare, one filled with desire, regret, and a tiny bit of sadness. It's an intense look that makes me swallow hard.

"Listen, I'm obviously not supposed to consort with the students here. I'm not even supposed to hang out with you guys beyond class time and meals. I can't go hang out with the boys and shoot hoops with them. I can't go and sit with you at the library and help you study. I can't do anything but teach and do crappy headmaster stuff. It's a shitty gig, but it's one I took willingly. You can imagine this job leaves me with absolutely no life. No relationships. No socialization beyond class time and conversations with other faculty."

"You can't even date the other staff?"

"First off, no, I'm their boss. Secondly, I don't want to. There's nobody here who appeals to me. Except one student, whom I can't have."

I swallow hard. "Me."

He nods. "Yes, you. There's something otherworldly drawing me to you, but I can't give in to it. That night a few months ago, it was a mistake. I succumbed to my desire to touch you, and in my defense, I'm just a regular twenty-eight-year-old guy. What red-blooded, straight male would have been able to just walk away from what I saw in front of me when I opened that door and saw you like that? So, I'm apologizing to you, Paige. It won't happen again."

I bite my lip and stare at the handsome headmaster. Wow, 28

years old, so young for such responsibilities. "What if I want it to?"

He sighs. "I know you want me to touch you again. I just can't. Besides, it seems you've got enough on your plate between the vampire, the dragon, and now this new warlock."

Wow, thanks for the slut-shaming. I grit my teeth. "Yeah, about that. Since you obviously know, I have to tell you that I'm confused about how they treat me. Jory and Breckon want to 'share' me. They also want to invite a third into our little group. Don't you think it's a bit weird?"

He grins. "You've never met polyamorous males before, have you?"

"Poly what?"

He leans forward, folds his hands on the desktop, and smiles. "Polyamorous. There are people in this world who don't like monogamy. They prefer to have relationships with more than one person at a time. This includes emotional and sexual. You're obviously not supposed to be having sexual contact with anyone at the school, so I'm going to skip over lecturing you on that part, because, while I know and enforce the rules, I cannot be everywhere at once. Just remember that the cameras are."

I resist an eye roll and make a gesture with my hand for him to continue.

"So, for argument's sake, you're in an emotional polyamorous relationship with Jory and Breckon. They want a third person to join, so there's four of you."

"Like, another girl?" I ask.

"Perhaps, but in this case, I believe it's another male they're wanting."

I cock my head to the side. "They've both told me they're straight. They're not into dudes at all. It's not like a third guy would be for them to have sex with, too."

"Some men enjoy watching the woman they love or care for get pleasured by other men. Not just one, or two."

I sniff. "I don't think I have the energy for that."

"Good, because you're not supposed to be doing anything sexual while you're here."

"Thanks for the reminder. Again," I mutter.

Griggs sighs again. "Paige, listen. I'm not stupid. I know shit goes on behind closed doors. A bunch of horny eighteen- to twenty-two-year-olds are not going to stay celibate for two years. The reason for that rule is to keep diseases and pregnancies out of this school. And relationship drama that interferes with learning. I'm assuming those boys brought condoms with them—smuggled them in somehow, because we don't provide them here. That would be condoning behavior that is forbidden."

I nod, understanding where he's coming from. "What about after I 'graduate' out of here?" I ask. "Could you and I have a relationship then? I'm just curious."

He shakes his head. "Not really. I'm committed to staying here as the headmaster. You need to move on with your life, go to a real college or a trade school. Find love. Find a career. What you have here with those boys—it's just fun to pass the time."

I frown, again, as he makes me feel like a fucking whore. I ignore that for now, because there's really nothing I can say to that. So I change the subject. "What made someone so young take on such a big responsibility?"

He smiles, but it doesn't quite reach his eyes. "Family business."

My eyes widen. "Really?"

He nods. "Yep. My uncle was the previous headmaster. When he announced his retirement, he begged me to take over for him, as he has no children of his own. In fact, I, myself, was a student here for two years, so I know what you're going through."

"You were? You broke three supernatural laws?" I ask, eyes wide.

He nods. "Yes, when I was eighteen, I spent two years here. It wasn't until about two years ago that I was offered the job. My uncle thought I was perfect for it because not only had I just received my bachelor's in Education, I had also been a student, so I would understand all the good—and the bad—that the students can get up to in here."

"Makes sense, I guess."

"So you can see, I'm kinda stuck here for the long haul."

"Doomed to be a terminal bachelor, forever single. No sex, no love, no having a family?"

He shrugs. "Maybe I'll try online dating. See if I can find a woman who wants to live in a secluded school in the Montana mountains with me for the next twenty years."

I laugh because it's the first time he's used wit and sarcasm around me. "Good luck with that." Then I think of something. "Where do you live, anyway? Here in the little town this school's in?"

He shakes his head. "No, I have my own faculties here on the grounds. As do all the staff. There's nothing around here for a hundred miles. The school provides us all we need in the way of food, clothing, shelter, and medical needs."

I frown. "Sounds like you're just as much a prisoner here as we are."

"Paige, you're not a prisoner. Stop thinking of it that way."

I sigh. "Fine."

"Again, I hope this stays between us and that I've cleared the air a little bit."

I tick off his bullet points with my fingers. "Yeah. You want me but can't have me, you're not going to touch me again, and I'm to remain celibate for the rest of my time here. Got it."

He smiles genuinely and it makes my heart melt. "Glad we understand each other."

Chapter 15

I walk into my dorm room to find Astrid sitting on the bed with the Stile in her hand. She drops it on the bed and grins wide as I walk in. "Don't leave out a single detail!" she squeals with a clap.

I throw my messenger bag on the bed and plop down on it with a sigh. Deciding to stay true to my word, I say, "He scolded me for the boob-flashing and told me not to do it again."

"That's it?" She frowns. "You were gone a while."

I nod. "Yeah. It was quite the lecture."

"Did he look at you all googly-eyed like he always does?" she asks, grinning.

"Yes, of course he did." I wish I could tell my bestie everything, but he took a chance confessing to me all of those personal things about him, so I can't really go and break my promise. I'll just keep it vague with her. It's bad enough she knows about his little visit to our room those months ago.

"Are you in trouble? Lose any points?"

I get up and hang my bag on the hook on the wall, and then begin stripping. I need a shower. "Nah. I didn't break any rules."

"What were you and Eliza talking about on the soccer field?"

I throw my shirt into the hamper and scowl. "She was supposed to pull her shirt up, too, but she either chickened out or wanted to frame me. I'm guessing it was the latter."

"But it was your choice, right? To flash Jory, and well, the whole team?" she asks meekly.

I nod. "Yes, as a distraction. To get him to miss the kick." I shrug. "Worked, I guess."

She laughs. "It did. He totally said the F-word, too. I'm sure he's glad it was too low for Fembot to hear."

I grin. "Good."

"We still lost the game though," she adds.

"Oh well," I say as I shut the bathroom door.

After a hot shower, I throw my wet hair into a messy bun and head off to meet Caleb at the library.

Caleb looks around. "I don't think we can make out in here, Witchy Spice. Too many cameras." He points to one in the corner.

I slap his arm with a snorting laugh. "I didn't invite you here to make out, silly. I need your help."

"With what?"

I drag the large book on witchcraft toward us, the one I found in the library's witchcraft section before he arrived, and open it up. I tap the page, "Locator spells. Do you know how to do those?"

He reads the first couple of paragraphs and then looks at me. "Nah, never learned 'em. I usually just have a dream if I need to find someone."

I raise an eyebrow. "You can just force your dreams to tell you?"

He shakes his head and then lifts the green and black Monster can to his lips before taking a swig. "No, if I really want to find something or someone, my subconscious knows. Then, I'll have a dream about it."

"Oh, okay," I say, disappointed, but keep reading.

"Why? Who are you trying to find?"

I look up from the page. "My grandmother's killer. The vampire."

"That's right, how could I forget?"

"My mom works for a vampire—it's his friend, or associate, or whatever that killed my gram."

His eyebrows hit his hairline. "Your mom works for a vamp? What does she do?"

I make a scoffing noise. "She's pretty da...rn vague about that, too. This and that, she says. Errands and stuff during the day when he doesn't want to go out. Legal documents, groceries, et cetera."

"When was your grandma killed?" He sets the can down and burps quietly.

"Couple of years ago," I reply.

I go on to tell him all I know.

"That sucks, girl. I'm sorry." He pulls me into a little side hug.

"Thanks. I know I can't do anything from here, but when I get out, my first priority is finding this bastard and ending him."

He makes a *tsking* sound of disapproval. "I don't know, honey. You might want to rethink that. If you think *this* prison is bad, you don't wanna go to real supernatural prison. It's pretty nasty there."

"How do you know?" I ask.

"My grandpa was in when he was younger. He told me stories. The human prisons are easier than the supernatural ones."

I don't even want to ask. "But this guy—this effing vampire—has to pay for what he did to my gram. He can't just get away with it." I smack my hand on the desk.

"Then call the supernatural cops. If we can prove it, they'll send him to prison. Like I said, it's *very* unpleasant."

I stare at my friend for a while. "Will he get a life sentence?"

He shrugs. "Not sure, but I can ask my pops when I call him next."

"Okay, just be careful. They monitor our cell phones."

"I don't have mine. I still use the stupid payphones." He rolls his eyes.

"I'm pretty sure they monitor those. too."

"I wouldn't doubt it. Now, let's try to figure out this locator spell and maybe we can find where he's at." He pulls the book toward him and begins to read. "Obviously, you don't have anything of his?"

I snort. "I don't even know his frickin' name."

"Okay." He continues to read and then stops suddenly, his finger on the page to keep his place. "Hey, do you have anything of your grandma's?"

I nod, pull her ring off, and hold it up to him.

Caleb takes it and inspects it. After placing it in the palm of his hand, he closes his fist and then his eyes. He mutters something I can't understand and then opens his eyes. A quick flash of purple colors his eyes before they go back to their warm caramel color. He hands me the ring back.

"What was that?" I gasp as I slip the ring back on my right-hand ring finger.

"I'll tell you in a second. Got a pic of your grand-mama?"

I nod and pull my cell phone out. I scroll through my gallery until I find one of her and me on my eighteenth birthday. I hand him the phone.

He whistles lowly. "Dang. Hot granny."

I chuckle. "Yeah, she definitely wasn't your rocking-chair-porch-knitting type."

"Are those real?" he asks, pointing at her cleavage.

I slap his hand with a laugh. "Yes, now stop."

His smile fades as he stares at the photo. He enlarges it with his fingers so only Gram's face is in the window. He again closes his eyes and mutters something, then quickly opens them to a flash of purple.

"What was her name?" he asks.

"Elizabeth Rawlings," I reply.

He nods and hands the phone back to me. "I've never tried this before, but I'm attempting to commit her to memory. Maybe if she sinks into my subconscious, I'll have a nice little dream about her."

"You mean about her murder?" I ask, eyebrow raised.

"Hopefully." He shrugs.

In the meantime, we study the locator spell, trying to figure out how to work it once we get a lock on this murderous leech.

After taking my seat in the Occult Studies classroom, I notice the word *DEMONS* is written across the whiteboard.

"Oh, goody," I snark under my breath. Demon lore. Yawn.

This class has been hard because I've been purposely avoiding Jory and Breckon and I have them both in this class. What Griggs said about them using me while I'm here hasn't left my brain, and I don't want to feel dirtier than I already do about how they've used me. I mean, it's not like I didn't get anything out of it myself, but it's just best if I avoid them for now. I need to be good and concentrate on getting a weekend pass so I can visit my mom and try to get some juice on this vamp who killed my gram.

"Take your seats, class," Mr. Johnson says, and I notice he's still in his gym teacher clothes. Must suck to have to teach two subjects, but it's not like this is a big school.

Once the class quiets down, he says, "Happy Monday, everyone. This week, we learn about demons." He underlines the word twice on the whiteboard. "Who, besides Jaxon, can tell me a little bit about demons?"

Nobody raises their hand.

"Okay then, enthusiastic about this topic, are we?" Johnson chuckles.

I raise my hand.

"Paige?"

"Not about demons, but I have a question. What are you? Human?"

He grins. "No, Paige. I'm a warlock. All the instructors here are witches and warlocks. I thought you knew that?"

"Can't sense your own kind?" Eliza asks around a snigger.

I turn around. "Quiet, magic tits. No one's talking to you."

A few laughs and sniggers can be heard.

"Paige…" Mr. Johnson warns.

"Sorry," I say. "I was just curious. About the teachers."

Johnson's dark-brown eyes flash purple quickly, and the class gasps. It looked fucking wicked cool against his dark skin.

"How did you do that?" I ask, my eyes wide. "Since that only happens when we do magic."

"You learn to control it. Mr. Griggs will show you in Magic 101."

"Can't wait." *To see Griggs, that is.*

"Okay first off, are demons made or born?"

"Both," Jaxon replies.

"Correct." Johnson draws dots of bullet points under the word *demon*. "A demon is a soul who's died but has managed to inhabit the body of a human. The demon's immortal soul keeps the human alive for as long as he or she pleases."

"What, like instead of going to Hell?" Eliza asks.

Johnson shakes his head. "Not really Hell, more like Purgatory, where he or she will be judged to determine their soul's final destination. So, you can imagine that if a soul wants to stay on earth and not go to Purgatory, they will most likely inhabit a human body to avoid going there because they're probably headed downstairs, not upstairs."

Everyone sort of shrinks away from Jaxon, and he glances around the room nervously.

"However," Johnson continues, "if said demon manages to find a mate, he or she can procreate, producing demon offspring called 'lesser demons'. These offspring are basically human with some form of supernatural power."

"Like what?" Astrid asks.

"A little bit of mind control and a little extra physical strength is all I've seen." He turns to Jaxon. "Am I correct?"

He nods. "Yes, I'm a lesser demon. My mom's the demon. My dad's human. He has no idea what she is."

The class gasps and begins murmuring amongst each other.

"What is her plan to explain her immortality while he grows older?" Johnson asks.

He shrugs. "Beats me."

"Will Jaxon age as well?" I ask.

"Yes," Johnson answers. "Like I said, basically human with a few parlor tricks. Nothing more."

"Thanks," Jaxon says wryly.

Johnson chuckles. "Be lucky you're mostly human. I assume you used mind control on people in order to get sent here?" He stares at the demon. "I mean, of course you don't have to answer."

Jaxon slowly nods his white-blond head. "Something like that."

"Is your mom, like, evil?" Jory asks.

"Not really. I mean, she told me she killed someone when she was human and was sure she was headed for Hell one day. So, when she eventually died, she hopped into a young woman's body who was in the hospital dying from car accident wounds. She told me she'll dump the body and take her punishment once me and dad are dead and gone."

I thought that was pretty sad. Just because you kill someone doesn't make you automatically headed for eternity in Hell. There could have been lots of circumstances around what happened. It gets me curious, but I have enough on my plate at the moment to ask Jaxon any questions.

Johnson continues to write on the whiteboard with his bullet points. "For the sake of today's class, we'll be talking about regular demons and not lesser demons. We'll get to them tomorrow. So, demons are immortal, can bend people's minds and wills, have super-strength, quick healing, and black eyes. By the way—they *can* control when their eyes turn black."

"Question," I say.

"Go ahead, Paige."

"What happens to the person whose body they took?"

"Good question. The reason they can only take over a dying person is because their will is too weak to fight. Sometimes the person dies once the host takes over, sometimes it lives. However, once the demon's soul exits the body, the host automatically dies, if it hasn't already."

I'm starting to really hate demons. Not that I particularly liked them before. Jaxon seems cool and normal, but he's the only one I've met. That I know of, anyway.

"But demons can be killed. Can anyone guess how?"

"Beheading?" Eliza suggests.

"Like we discussed before, beheading anything will kill it. So, yes, you're right there, Eliza. Basically, they're like vampires. Destroy the heart or head and you have exorcised the demon."

"Will black smoke go flying out of their mouth like in the movies?" Astrid asks.

"Or pea soup vomit?" Jory asks, snickering.

The class laughs.

"No, it won't. The host will just drop dead. You won't see anything else." Johnson continues to write his bullet points about how to kill one.

I take notes. This is good stuff and will probably come in useful sometime in my life. Huh, I really am learning useful shit here. Who knew?

Chapter 16

I sit alone in the library, studying the witchcraft book. Astrid and Alicia are cramming for midterm exams we have in a few days, but I'm pretty sure I'll pass them with no issues. Math isn't a problem for me, just boring, and I've pretty much soaked up all the occult and magic stuff from the classes like a sponge because it's so interesting to me. Real-life stuff we'll need in our supernatural lives.

As I attempt to memorize some of the locator spell, I stop when I sense a presence looming on the other side of the table. I see the two boys I've been avoiding for weeks standing there, staring down at me, their faces serious.

"Mind if we sit?" Jory asks, touching the chair in front of him.

I look down at the book. "Yes. I mind."

They sit anyway.

I sigh and look at the two most handsome faces I've ever had the pleasure of kissing. "What do you guys want? I'm busy."

"Why have you been avoiding us, baby?" Breckon asks.

I stare into his dark eyes and see genuine curiosity and even concern there. "Listen, guys. Don't take it personal, okay? I'm just busy and think it's best if we stop hooking up. Eventually, we'll get caught and I really need that weekend pass. It was fun, but I'm sure you can find another girl to hook up with. I bet Eliza would be game." Even as the words tumble from my mouth, I feel my heart breaking and jealousy simmering. I don't want either one of them touching or even looking at her. Or any other girl for that matter. But they seem intent on having their poly-whatever fun.

Jory looks around the quiet and mostly deserted library and

then grabs my hand. "Paige, we aren't just 'hooking up' with you. We want you. We need you. Both of us do."

"Yes," Breckon adds. "Not just your body. It's your mind. Your heart. Your soul. All of you."

I shake my head to try to clear it, as this is in direct contrast to what Griggs had said. I fight back tears because I miss them both so much.

But... I tend to believe Griggs more than these guys because he's older and it sounded like he was speaking from experience. I plaster on my best smile. "Look, guys. I know that dudes have to say what they have to in order to keep a girl sleeping with them. I totally get it, and, hey, no hard feelings. Really. But you can be honest with me because I already know this is just fun to pass the time. You guys are into group hookups. I was game, I have a nice body, and I'm not shy. I get why you want to keep me. But I cannot risk getting any more points taken, or I'd continue helping you pass the time by"—I drop my voice to a bare whisper—"fucking and sucking our way to graduation. It's not that I haven't had fun, I totally have, but—"

Before I can even finish my sentence, Breckon uses his vampire speed to lift me from my chair and push me up against a stack of books inside the closest book aisle. His hand is around my throat, not hard enough to cut off my breathing, but to show control.

I gasp in surprise, my eyes wide.

He leans down and whispers in my ear, "Paige, you aren't fucking getting it. This isn't playtime for us. This isn't just bored hookups to pass the time. Jory and I fucking love you and you are ours. You understand? *Ours*. We need you, we want you, and we cannot and will not be with anyone else." He finishes by licking my neck and then jamming his fangs into my carotid, causing me to exhale a sharp gasp.

I become languid under him and my panties are about to go up in proverbial flames. I groan softly when I feel Jory kissing the other side of my face and then down my neck.

Breck quickly retracts his fangs and reaches up to kiss me on the mouth while using his hand to grip my cheeks. It's mind-numbing, and once he breaks the kiss, he says, "Mine, Paige. You're mine." Jory pushes him out of the way and kisses me as well, his hot body heat almost making me sweat—since I'm already hot. I moan under his searing kiss. Jory breaks from me and I whimper at the loss. He whispers against my lips, "Mine, Paige, you're fucking mine."

As they step back, they both stare at me. Breckon takes a quick look both ways down the book aisle then back to me. "Do you understand now, baby?"

I nod slightly and lick my lips, wide-eyed and speechless.

"You're ours. His and mine." He points to Jory, then himself. "And once we find a third, you'll be theirs, too."

My eyebrows raise. "Why can't it just be you two?"

I hear the librarian calling out for me, probably wondering where I went since I left the book open and my messenger bag on the chair.

"It has to be three, Paige. Three," Jory responds before they both disappear on the other side of the stack and out of sight.

I straighten my skirt and tie, smooth down my hair, wipe off my mouth, and walk out of the aisle wondering what the fuck just happened and if I have a change of underwear in my bag.

"Are you serious?" Astrid gasps at the lunch table while Alicia and Rainlily are still grabbing their lunches. They have obviously seen the way the dragon and vampire flirt with me, and I shared a little about how they're both "into" me, but they don't need to know all the filthy, dirty details.

"Yep," I say, standing outside the lunchroom waiting for the other two girls so we can eat at one of the park benches. It's too nice to eat our bagged meals inside.

"I just don't understand the 'three' thing," she comments as she peeks inside the bag to see what's for lunch.

"Me either, but they keep saying it." I want to tell her about how I asked Griggs about it, but I can't. So I reply, "I still think it's just a ruse to keep me coming back for more. I think they're polys." I hope that's a word because I couldn't remember the real word Griggs used.

"Polys?" Astrid looks at me questioningly.

"What are polys?" Rainlily asks, obviously too quiet for her own good since I hadn't heard her or Alicia approach.

Damn ninjas.

We go sit on the benches and open up our bags. Deciding that, as long as I keep myself out of the story, I'll be okay to talk about it. "Oh, we were just talking about that sex thing where people are into doing it with more than one person at a time."

"That's just, like, an orgy," Alicia says.

I raise my eyebrows at her. "I thought it was poly something."

She takes out her wrapped peanut butter and jelly sandwich and says, "No. Polyamorous is where more than three or more people are in an actual relationship, all with each other. They have feelings for each other, usually are in love, and of course, the, uh, sex follows."

I look at the other two and point to the quiet witch. "Check out this girl and her encyclopedia of sexual facts!"

They laugh, including Alicia. "I'm really not an encyclopedia, I was just watching this show about it on TV a couple years ago and it intrigued me." She smiles before she bites into her sandwich.

"Why are we talking about this?" Rainlily asks, popping open a bag of chips.

I have to think of something fast. So, I shrug casually. "Overheard some people talking about it. Just wondered what it was." I hold up my phone. "No time to Google, ya know."

Thankfully, the subject changes to classes, demons, Magic 101, and eventually lands on how hot Headmaster Griggs is. I agree with the girls and wish I could tell them his sad story of being stuck as headmaster out of familial duty and how he, himself, was a student here once. But of course, I keep my mouth shut and stick to the shallow details about how gorgeous he is, how he looks in gray sweatpants, and then guessing on whether or not he's packing anything impressive behind them.

They say men are bad with their locker-room talk. Women are *so* much worse.

Chapter 17

Headmaster Anton Griggs

I sit staring at the stack of papers I need to grade, but my mind is elsewhere. And honestly, I'm pissed off.

Pissed as fuck at myself for letting it get as far as it did with Paige. I should have *never* given in when I caught her about to fuck the dragon shifter. My jealousy had roared beneath the surface, the green monster egging me on when I saw him sneak into the female dorm building. I'm no fool. I knew exactly where he was headed. I knew he had a thing for my Paige, and that she was into him, too. I should have just let it happen, both at the pool house the first time, and again in her dorm. But I just couldn't.

Why am I so upset at the thought of them hooking up? If I thought it was just mindless sex, then I would have let it go. Gritted my teeth and turned a blind eye. Kids will be kids. They're horny and just coming into their sexuality and shit happens. It's why I turn a blind eye to the rest of the crap that goes on here when it comes to sex. I lied to Paige when I told her I assumed they'd snuck in the condoms. I *knew* those boys had them. All the boys do. Better safe than sorry. If I pretend I don't know, then it's not implied consent. Right?

I push a few buttons on my keyboard to put the male and female dorms on separate screens. I want to see if Paige goes in, or if the dragon or vampire goes out. At this time of night, it means nothing but sex.

I lift the scotch to my lips and take a sip. I'm glad the Academy's board of directors hooked me up with this home office here in the small house they built as the headmaster's quarters a couple of acres past the school. They wanted me so bad, I made them build me my own house—to my specifications. Panic room, basement, home office, luxury kitchen, state-of-the-art security system. Sure, it's only about 1,500 square feet, but it's perfect for me and keeps me comfortable. Especially since it's the only thing I have to look forward to at the end of a long day. I wasn't lying to Paige when I told her I was alone out here. No relationships. No friends. No social life. Just teaching and running this place.

With my feet up on the desk, I sip my scotch and watch the monitors. I can grade those papers, but I'd rather see what goes on in the dorms. A figure in a hoodie sneaks by the camera and disappears out of sight. Too bad they don't know there's a pinhole camera installed in the wall, parallel to the door handle of the dorm. It points right at a person's face. I frown when I see Jack McAllister's face on the screen as he enters the girls' dorms.

"Have fun getting laid," I grumble dryly to the warlock on the screen, lifting my glass in salute. I can't remember which vampire girl he's fucking, but it's irrelevant. No pregnancies or diseases will result, so I brush it off.

My mind drifts back to the day when Astrid Marx came into my office unannounced. Yvette had been out, and Astrid walked in to talk to me about her grade in one of her classes. I'd been re-watching the footage of Paige and Jory Erickson in the pool room, about to fuck, and I couldn't help myself. My dick had been rock-hard, watching my Paige about to get pleasured by the dragon shifter. Thank God my back had been turned and I'd been able to tuck it back in my pants before turning around. I still, to this day, wonder if Astrid suspected anything—and more importantly, if she told Paige. I couldn't worry about it, though. Nothing I can do about it now.

Movement on the fourth monitor catches my eye. This is the camera I have mounted outside my own house. Shock flashes through me when I see two men at my front door. The doorbell resounds seconds after I see one of them pushing its button on the cameras. I squint to see that the two resemble Jory Erickson and Breckon Dash.

What the hell?

I set my bourbon down and slip on a T-shirt before making my way to the door. I cautiously open it and see the dragon shifter and vampire standing there.

"Gentlemen, what are you doing here?" I ask them.

Breckon glances around and then to me. "Can we come in? We need to talk to you."

"My office hours are posted on the office door, come see me tomorrow."

I go to close the door, but Jory's hand stops its movement. "This isn't school business."

As I stare into both their eyes, I can see they are dead serious. I nod slightly and open the door, inviting them in with a wave of my hand.

The living room greets us, and I indicate for them to sit. They take a seat on the couch, while I stand, my arms folded. "My first question is—how do you know where I live? If you don't answer me, I'm going to ask you both to leave. No discussion."

Jory glances at Breckon. "We had you followed one day after school. But honestly, I think a lot of students know these homes are out here. People get bored and go exploring. My first thought was faculty homes when I first came upon this little area."

"Fine. Now what do you need?" I ask.

"We're here about Paige Masset," the vampire answers.

I try to resist looking surprised, so I clamp my jaw together.

At my non-answer, he continues, "We know you have a thing for the witch."

I raise an eyebrow. "What the fuck makes you say that?"

Both boys smile, most likely at my profanity. It's a double-standard thing with me. I can do it, the students fucking can't.

"Caleb Owens told us. He puts his paws all over her in front of you. Flirts with her while you're watching. He told us you look like you want to murder him when he does it."

"He's wrong," I deadpan. But inside, I've already flunked the flamboyant warlock from passing Magic 101 for his deception.

"He's not," Breckon says boldly. "Caleb was paid to tell us the truth. He has no reason to lie. We obviously aren't allowed to take the magic classes, and he's been reporting back to us."

"What the fuck do you want?" I finally ask, already tired of their haughtiness and the disruption to my evening.

Jory asks, "Sir, do you love Paige?"

"No more than I love any of my students," I reply, raising my chin.

"Liar." Breckon pierces me with his dark, narrowed stare.

That pisses me off. "I beg your pardon? You asked me a question, I answered it. You don't get to call me a liar."

"Okay, it's time to cut to the chase," Jory says to Breckon, then puts his attention back to me. "Listen, Anton. Can I call you Anton?"

"No," I seethe.

"Okay, Mr. Griggs, here's the deal. We think we've found a way to unlock the Coresh Accord."

The fuck...?!

Maintaining my composure becomes difficult. "You've done *what*?"

Breckon pulls his phone from his pocket, and after a few taps, he begins to read from it. "The Coresh Accord states that under the fourth full moon of the twenty-first year of the century, a romantic and sexual relationship between four supernaturals will occur, one female, three males. Two can be of any race, but one male and the female must be of the same race. Once this union ensues, the Coresh Accord can therefore be unlocked, granting all four immortality. If any of the parties does not have true, pure love for the female, the spell will not work." Breckon looks up at me. "We believe you are the fourth. Paige, me, Jory... we need you to unlock this spell."

"You already have immortality. Sort of," I say to the vampire.

Breckon shakes his head. "Nah, we just age really slow. I'm not trying to get old, gray, and need Viagra, if you know what I'm sayin'."

"So you *forced* yourselves to love Paige just to unlock this spell? I'm not buying it." I narrow my eyes at them.

I learned about the Coresh Accord in college, but I had also heard about it growing up. It was always considered an old wives' tale and I never bothered studying up on it. It was literally one question on my occult studies test in college. Haven't thought about it since.

"No, that's not how this went down at all," Jory starts. "We both fell in love with Paige the minute we laid eyes on her. Like she put us under some spell. We were actually worried she might have."

"She's not that powerful or schooled in magic," I say dryly, my arms still folded across my chest.

"We realize that now. Especially with Caleb in our back pocket. He told us she's totally into us, and has also revealed she doesn't know much more than a few party tricks when it comes to magic." Jory leans forward and folds his hands over his knees.

"That part is true," I say, wishing I wouldn't have left my scotch in the office. I eye the liquor cabinet and go to it. "Go on."

Breckon sighs and pierces me with his dark gaze. "Listen,

you probably know that Breck and I have been friends for a while. We didn't plan on coming here to try to unlock some damn spell. We came here to do our time and then move the fuck on. But when we met Paige, it was instant. We discussed it at first, trying to decide which one of us was gonna get to pursue her. But neither of us could give her up. We made the decision to share her—and honestly, we've shared girls in the past. But just for fun. Hookups and fuck-girls. But that's when the Coresh Accord came to mind. I heard warlocks talking about that shit the county jail the first time I was arrested. When I got out, I researched it. It intrigued me, but then I forgot about it, since I'm not a witch and didn't know any. Not really."

I pour some whiskey into my glass and then throw it back. I quickly pour another. "Go on."

"Look, man. We know it's against the rules, or whatever, to be with a student. But we know you want her. Just by the look on your face we can tell you're in love with her. We gotta make this happen." Breckon stands and runs his fingers through his hair. "You're a warlock, she's a witch. There's the two of the same race the spell mentions. Jory and I are the other two. It's easy. April twenty-sixth is the fourth full moon of the twenty-first year. We have to perform the fuckin' spell."

"Why don't you just use Caleb?" I ask, immediately feeling rage bubble at the thought of him putting his dick anywhere near her. Loving her. "He's a warlock."

"Nope," Breckon responds. "He's not in love with her. We asked."

"What about Jack McAllister?" I suggest.

"Again," Jory says. "He doesn't love her. Doesn't even look her way. I've watched him, because I thought of him, as well. I think he's in love with Eliza Morris, anyway."

After what I saw on the cameras earlier, he's definitely putting it on someone in the female dorms.

"You gotta understand the stipulations of the spell. We all

have to be in love with her. You can't force that." Jory sighs.

I down my second glass and rake my fingers through my hair for the hundredth time. My problem isn't being in a polyamorous relationship, because honestly, it's always been a fantasy of mine. A strong desire, actually. My problem is my position. I'm the fucking headmaster, for God's sake. How do I even hide the fact that I'm with a student? Which reminds me…

"If I agree to this—and I probably don't need to ask—but it's just us and her, right? Neither of you are into dudes?"

They both shake their heads.

"Nah. Are you?" Jory asks.

"No. Not that I care if other people are into it, I'm just not. I would want the focus to be on Paige."

"Agreed." Breckon sits back down and looks at his phone once more. "So, the spell to complete the immortality portion is here, but it needs two witches to perform it. Can you and Paige pull it off?

I set my glass down and nod. "Yeah, between her grandmother's spellbook she stole out of my office, and my many resources, we can pull it off no problem."

"Caleb offered to help with the spell, too."

I nod. More hands on deck won't be a bad thing. He already knows everything, anyway, apparently.

The two boys fist-bump each other and then step closer to me. They both put out their hands. "Let's make this official." I shake both their hands and they smile from ear to ear.

I can't help but smile, too. Excitement, lust, and dread all swirl inside of me. What in the hell have I gotten myself into?

Chapter 18

Paige

I watch in awe as Alicia pulls water up from the stream and swirls her finger, causing a funnel to form in the palm of her hand. "Beautiful," I breathe.

The class cranes their necks back to watch the water funnel grow taller and bigger, stretching toward the sky.

Suddenly, the funnel collapses, and half the students are splashed with water. Alicia gasps in shock. I look around to see Caleb laughing, his hand over his mouth.

"What did you do?" I ask.

"Mr. Owens, see me after class," Headmaster Griggs says, murder coloring his features.

"A-yes, sir," he replies in a high-pitched Southern accent.

The class shuffles away from the stream and back toward the clearing in the forest.

I grab Caleb by the arm and yank him toward a nearby tree. We're doing outdoor magic again for Magic 101, and I didn't want us to risk getting put back on classroom time. "Why did you do that?"

"To get you alone." Caleb waggles his eyebrows.

"Bullshit," I whisper. "Spill, now."

He glances toward the class then back to me.

"No, seriously. I wanted to talk to you." His eyes search mine.

"Why?" I flick my gaze behind me at the group, then back at him. "About what?"

"Are you into him? The headmaster?" he asks.

I look away, letting go of my grip on the cute warlock. "It's nothing more than a little teacher crush."

"I'm calling bullshit, girlfriend," he whispers in my ear.

I pull away from him and say, "It doesn't matter. Let's go back to class."

It was his turn to grab my arm before I could storm off. I look down at his grip on my bicep and furrow my brow. "Let go of me, Caleb."

"Answer me," he hisses.

I laugh at his demand. "Why do want to know?"

"I *need* to know." He lessens his grip. "Just tell me."

I sigh, sliding my hand over the top of my head and then gripping my ponytail at the base. "Look, yeah, I may get a little starry-eyed when he's teaching, or when he's around. But I don't think I'm in love with the guy. That's ridiculous. I've only had a handful of interactions with him."

"You know you can love someone from the first time you lay eyes on them," he reminds me.

"Yeah, yeah. Love at first sight. Blah, blah. Why do you even care?" I pierce him with a demanding stare.

"Maybe I'm jealous," he suggests with a grin.

"Again, bullshit. You just want to fuck me. You have no feelings for me."

"The first part is true. You have a smokin' bod." His gaze roams my body from top to bottom. "I won't comment on the second part. Just know, Paige, that there are a lot of dudes at this school who are looking to score with you."

"What?" That can't be true. I only know of my dragon, vampire, and the headmaster. And dammit, that's more than exhausting as it is.

"It is. Now, let's get back to class." Caleb drops a quick kiss on my head.

The headmaster eyes us both as we re-join the circle, and the way Griggs's stare locks on mine a little longer than appropriate, I begin to wonder if he meant anything he said during our one-on-one meeting a few days ago. About how he can't be with me, about how he can't have any interaction with the students. About how he needs to stay professional and just run the school and have no life. By the way he's looking at me now, he wants to fuck me ten ways to Sunday.

I certainly wouldn't object.

The fact he told me he won't be with me just makes me want him more. It's in my rebellious nature and it's probably the worst thing he could have told me. It's like he's a challenge now. One I know I need to give up on. I've got enough dicks pointed at me at the moment. My heartrate increases and my panties melt at the way his eyes are boring into mine.

"Earth magic is strong but delicate," Griggs begins, breaking the stare and turning his teacher mode back on. "It's a balance you have to master before you can use it. For instance." He walks to the lone yellow dahlia and crouches down. "Grow and reproduce, little flower. Let the light of the sun and the showers of the heavens make you fruitful and multiply." He closes his eyes as his hand hovers over the delicate dahlia.

We all wait for something to happen to the flower, but nothing does. He rises from his crouched position and returns to the circle. "Earth magic also requires patience. We'll check on little miss dahlia in a couple days."

Well, that was anticlimactic.

"Paige, come to the center of the circle, please."

I walk to the center and stand, waiting for instruction. "I'm here, Headmaster."

He points to the ground, where there is nothing but pine

needles and sticks. "Create a bonfire."

I know to manipulate fire, but there has to be fire there to manipulate. But I just answer, "Yes, Headmaster."

I stare at the ground, and then I have an idea. Griggs let us bring our class-issued Stiles with us, so I draw the rune of speed on my arm. Once done, I drop the Stile to the ground, lean down, and pick up two small sticks. With my enhanced speed, I rub the sticks together until they're nothing more than a blur. Smoke begins to billow from the friction, and pretty soon, sparks fly. It's not long until a small flame forms. I drop the sticks and a lazy fire begins to grow. I know that I don't have hours to wait for a bonfire to grow, so I draw another small rune of speed on my arm. With vampire swiftness, I dart back and forth between the clearing and the trees, gathering wood and sticks to build my bonfire. Within ninety seconds, we have a raging bonfire.

*Ooh*s and *ahh*s can be heard and the students begin to walk closer, wanting the warmth from the fire on this chilly March afternoon.

"Simply amazing," Griggs says in my ear as the rest of the students are distracted by the fire. I look up into his face and smile. "Thank you, Headmaster."

"We need to talk, Paige. And soon."

"I thought we already did that," I reply, confused.

He doesn't answer me, but walks to the center of the clearing. He pulls a bag of marshmallows, chocolate bars, and graham crackers from his backpack and tells us the snack is a reward for our hard work, and that we'll enjoy the rest of the class having a treat.

Despite the hot interaction with the duo in the library, I've still mostly been avoiding the dragon and the vampire. I still don't believe they want anything more than a fun way to pass the time here. Who this 'third' they want to join us was, I'm not sure. But I know it's not Caleb because he's cooled his pursuit of me and is now heavily flirting with a known gay shifter we have in math class.

Sure, we're still friends, but I think that's how I want to keep it. Caleb's a cool guy and I sure appreciate his psychic ability and his willingness to help me find my grandmother's killer. However, according to him, he still hasn't had any dreams about her or her murderer. I'm a patient girl, I can wait. That doesn't mean I'm not going to do my own research, though.

"Do you have any locator spells in your spellbook?" I ask Astrid as I flip through my own, sitting cross-legged on my bed.

She nods. "There's one in here, but it seems to only work on locating humans."

I look up from my book. "What? That's stupid."

She lifts a shoulder and lets it fall. "Don't know why. I didn't write the dang thing."

I huff out a noise of disappointment and continue poring over my grandmother's spellbook. Now, *my* spellbook.

"Go ahead, keep it," my mom says as she rushes out the door. "I was never much interested in learning all the spells, anyway. My mother had her own special way of doing magic—one I couldn't quite understand and don't have time to learn."

Mom closes the door behind her, and I'm left alone in the house. I stare down at the spellbook and wonder if I can decipher any of the spells in there. I thumb through it, and admittedly, the spells are pretty complex. Maybe she wrote them that way on purpose. Or maybe I'm just a dumbass.

All night long I study the book. Read it from front to back. I'm not sure I retained much, but I do know that some of the spells clicked in my pea brain. The night of studying exhausts me, and I fall asleep with the book open, across my chest, my hand protectively covering it.

I sigh at the high school-era memory and keep flipping. As I'm almost to the back, I see a spell in small writing called the Coresh Accord. Why does that sound familiar to me?

"What the hell is this?" I murmur.

"What?" Astrid asks.

I hold the book up, and my bestie squints at the words. "The Coresh Accord." She snorts. "It's a sex spell."

I gasp. "What?"

"Funny that we were just having the polyamorous conversation today because I think that spell has something to do with that."

My stomach churns, but not in a good way. There's an odd feeling of dread there. I swallow hard. "Are you serious?"

She nods and begins flipping through her own spellbook. When she doesn't find what she's looking for, she pulls out her cell phone and begins typing. While she thumb-scrolls, I look down at my own book and read the spell. *Four star-crossed lovers, under the fourth full moon of the twenty-first year, will find love with each other, for all eternity.*

"What the hell…" I whisper.

"Here it is," Astrid says. "Three male supernaturals must secure the love of one female supernatural under the full moon in the fourth month of the twenty-first year. One of the male supernaturals must be of the same race as the female. The other two may be of any supernatural race. Unlock the spell and they will find eternal love with each other."

I swallow hard and then want to puke.

"There must be three."

Is this what Breckon meant?

I glance at the date on my phone. March 7th, 2021. The fourth full moon of the year is next month—end of April.

"Astrid... uh... I think I have a problem."

Chapter 19

Annoyed, I sit in Griggs's office, once again. "You said we needed to talk. Again. What is it now?"

He stares at me hard and then opens his mouth to speak before shutting it again.

"Cat got your tongue?" I lift an eyebrow and fold my arms across my chest.

"No." He blows out a breath and stands up. He turns around and touches the book *A Case for Witches*. The bookcase slides aside to reveal a hidden passage.

He turns around, watching me.

With a deadpan expression, I look at him. "Oh, my God, you have a hidden passage," I exclaim, monotone.

"Cut the shit, Paige, I know you've been back here. Stole your grandmother's spellbook and whatever else from your purse. Come on."

He climbs through the back and I don't rise from my seat. What good is going to come from me exploring this secret cove with him? He's made it clear he doesn't want a relationship with me, nor will he touch me again. I got what I wanted from my handbag and have no interest in anything down there. Is he going to kill me and hide my body behind that bookcase?

"What are you waiting for?" he asks, popping his head out and staring at me.

I shake my head. "I'll pass, Headmaster."

He crawls out and stands fully upright at six-foot-two. "Get your ass up, Paige." He puts his hand out.

Surprised by his aggressiveness, and liking it, I stand and

reach for his proffered hand. He grips mine and leads me behind the bookcase. The simple connection of touch sends sparks of excitement through me. I swallow hard while I grip Griggs's hand tight.

We slowly descend the staircase and reach the area where the students' personal effects are stored. It smells like a mixture of dampness and campfire down here.

I look past the items and see some kind of a rock pile. He leads me further into the darkness before pulling a lighter from the pocket of his trousers. He quickly brings it up to a sconce on the wall. A flame flares to life on a torch inside the sconce and rewards us with light.

I can now see that the pile of rocks is an altar of some kind. I spy evidence of a recent fire by the char marks on the top of it. A few burnt leaves and some ash are all that's left from whatever ritual or sacrifice was performed here.

"What do you do with this?" I ask, pointing at it.

"This is where I practice magic. Spells and incantations. It's quiet and nobody disturbs me," he answers.

I stare at the altar in the bouncing flames from the torch. "Why are you showing me this?"

"Jory and Breckon came to see me last night," he says.

My eyes dart to his and my eyes widen. "What… why…?"

Griggs pulls his hand out of his pocket and grabs my other one. He stares down at me, and asks, "Are you in love with those boys?"

I flick my gaze between both his eyes and stare up at him.

How do I answer that?

Yes, I've been pretty depressed the past couple of weeks, having avoided the duo. I would be lying if I said I didn't miss their looks, their attention, their fiery touches. Sadly for me, none of my feelings for them has changed. In fact, they're stronger, if that's possible.

But is it love?

"The truth is—I don't know. I've never been in love before, so I don't know how to answer that. It started off as a crush, but it's been developing into more." Then something occurs to me. "You asked me with a straight face if I was in love with two guys. You don't find that, like, odd?"

Griggs shakes his head and gently caresses the back of my hand with his finger. The touch is so light, yet arousing. I have to control my breathing as his baby-blues pierce my soul. "No, because those boys are polyamorous. Like we discussed."

My eyebrows rise. "They told you that?"

He nods. "Yes, Paige. They did. They've shared women in the past, but you're... different."

"So I've been told," I murmur and then look down.

Griggs uses the tip of his finger to tilt my chin up. "You *are* different. You're the one. You're her."

I shake my head slightly. "I'm who?"

"The one to fulfill the Coresh Accord."

What the...?

Realization dawns. "Oh, my God. I was just reading about that yesterday. I thought it was bullshit."

I slap my hand over my mouth.

Griggs chuckles. "No speakers down here."

I relax. "Thank fuck."

He laughs again. "You wanna know a secret? I created that female voice. With magic. There really are no speakers."

I arch an eyebrow. "Really? Because in our dorm room we can cuss, nothing happens. Nor when we whisper."

"The spell is only active in the main parts of the school.

Classrooms, lunchroom, gym, hallways, et cetera."

I bite my lip and stare up at him. "Why are you telling me this?"

He ignores my question. "Back to the Coresh Accord... I'm going to teach you how to perform the spell."

I raise a hand. "Hold up. I'm confused. Astrid said it was some kind of sex spell. From what I feel brewing between us, we don't need one," I proclaim boldly, hoping he feels the same.

He shakes his head. "It's not a sex spell. It's an immortality spell."

A gasp spills from my lips. "Wha... what?"

He quickly goes over what Astrid had told me about the fourth month of the twenty-first year, but he continues more in-depth about how the males must love the female or the spell won't work.

I'm pacing as he talks, my finger to my mouth because this is all just so... so... I have no words.

"So, what you're saying is that you, Breckon, and Jory are *in love* with me?"

With his hands in his pants pockets, he curtly nods once. "Yes."

I whoosh out a breath and stop pacing. "What if I'm not in love with all of you?"

He narrows his eyes at me. "I actually don't think it matters—as far as the spell's concerned. That being said, I already know you feel something for the vampire and the dragon shifter. And I sure as fuck know you want me."

I shove my hands on my hips and arch an eyebrow. "Is that so?"

He nods. "Yes, and on April twenty-sixth, the four of us are going to come down here and perform the spell to activate the Coresh Accord."

I shake my head. "Wait, I still don't understand. What does the spell do?"

"It'll grant the four of us immortality. We'll be able to be together forever."

The way he says it, combined with the look of adoration in his eyes, is beyond romantic. So, of course, since feelings have made an appearance in the room, I have to pop off with, "And what if I don't want to deal with all your asses for eternity?"

He chuckles and grabs my hand. "Too bad. We want you and nobody else can have you."

He leads me away from the altar and past the personal effects. I see my pink and white purse lying there but pay it no mind. I already got out of it what I needed.

"So much shit down here. You should at least let people have their purses and backpacks."

"We provide backpacks to the guys and messenger bags to the girls. What do they need this stuff for?" He sweeps his arm around the room.

I roll my eyes and slap his arm. "Because. We just do."

Griggs stops and turns to me. "Do you know why we confiscate personal belongings when students first come here?"

"Because you guys are dicks?" I suggest, blinking up at him innocently.

He grins. "We are dicks, but that's not the real reason."

I shrug and look past him at all the backpacks, purses, and bags. "Good to know."

Griggs grips my face with his fingers and makes me look at him. "We do it because we care. We want you to succeed here. We don't want you having access to anything that will harm or distract you, your fellow students, or the faculty."

I want to snap my head out of his grip, but I resist. "Such as?"

"Spellbooks, for one."

I swallow hard and stare up into his scrutinizing gaze. It's so dark down here, I can't see the blue in his irises. "What are you talking about?"

"Cut the crap, Paige. I know you took your book out of your purse. I know you broke in here—you and Astrid. You don't think I have cameras in my fucking office? I have them everywhere."

My eyes widen and I shake my head to try to recover. "Still don't know what you mean, Headmaster."

"Goddamn it, you're so infuriating!" he roars, pushing me back against the wall.

His anger both scares and excites me. I decide I should probably leave and head for the staircase. I shake off his hold on me and flick a hand at him. "Dude, bye."

I don't make it ten steps before he's turning me around then pushing me up against the cold stone wall of this dungeonlike storage space.

"Why did you bring me here, Anton?" I try using his first name to get his attention.

"To talk to you about the spell. And then… once you and I come to an agreement… to fuck you," he whispers against my lips, his breath washing over me.

Oh, hell…

"I thought you said that was off-limits," I pant, wide-eyed.

He pushes his body against mine and I can feel his stiff cock pushing into my stomach. "It is, but I can't stay away from you. It's physically impossible." He leans down and presses his mouth to mine. I gasp in surprise but quickly recover by kissing him back. Holy hell, is he an outstanding kisser.

His hands reach down and pulls open my uniform shirt. The buttons go flying all over the stone floor. *Plink-plink-plink.*

My sweater comes off next and falls to the floor. In just my necktie, skirt, and bra, Griggs lifts me up and I straddle his waist, groaning at the feel of his rock-hard dick pressing against the damp heat of my panties. I roll my hips to gain friction as he reaches inside my bra to fondle my nipple. I whimper against his mouth and continue bucking my hips against him.

"Fuck, Paige," he says as he breaks the kiss and presses his forehead against mine. He lifts my sports bra off over my head and tosses it to the floor.

In the bouncing candlelight from the walls, I can see the look of indecision and lust dancing in his gaze. "I want you so fucking bad," he whispers.

"Then take me," I breathe in reply.

"You good with this?" he asks between breaths. "We agree that you're going to be with the three of us?"

I nod. "Yes, I agree."

He leans down and presses another toe-curling kiss to my lips.

I unbutton his shirt and slide it off his shoulders, where it flutters to the ground. Next is his belt buckle and the button and zipper of his pants. He sets me down as he kicks out of his shoes, then pants, leaving him in only his boxer briefs.

Deciding to help him with those, I kneel down and slide them off his hips. I'm rewarded with a thick, beautiful cock bouncing in my face.

"Mmm," I say as I lick the bottom of the shaft.

Anton shudders hard and grips my hair. "Oh, God."

I take him in my mouth and then pull off to lick slowly up the shaft again.

"Suck my balls," he commands.

I do as he says, pulling one into my mouth, grateful he's the keep-it-hairless type. Not that I've sucked many balls in my life, but the thought of hairy ones is just… yuck.

I rake my nails over the other one as I let go of his testicle and insert his thick, throbbing member into my mouth. He hisses out his approval and grips my ponytail in his fist. I love how he tries to control the movement of my head, when I'm the one really in control. I just let him think he is.

I can feel his cock swelling in my mouth and I smile around it. My fingers are fondling his balls, my nails scraping gently on his taint.

"Fuck, Paige, stop, or I'm gonna come."

I pull off his dick with a sucking-pop and smile up at him. "Isn't that the idea… Headmaster?"

"At this point, you're the *head*master," he hisses.

He pulls me up by my hand and pushes my back against the wall again. He lifts my skirt and then hoists me up by my ass so I have to wrap my legs around his waist. The minute they do, his cock is instantly thrust inside me.

"Oh, God," I whimper, my head slamming back against the wall.

"I don't know how long I can last, baby girl," he whispers against my mouth. "It's been so long, and your cunt is so tight."

But he doesn't stop his aggressive pace, thrusting his hips hard and fast against me as the friction of his swollen cock rubs against my g-spot. I grip my fingers on his shoulders, my nails digging in.

My climax is close, and when he breaks our kiss to lean down and suck one nipple into his mouth, I cry out. An orgasm slams into me so hard, I see stars.

"Oh, shit," he groans, right as he stills his plunging, his seed spurting deep inside my wet heat. He jerks a couple more times, thrusting while milking his cock inside me until I doubt a drop is left.

He lets go of me and I can barely stand. I feel dizzy and breathless. He slides his shorts and pants back on and picks me up, where he carries me up the stairs.

Chapter 20

Anton

Coffee cup in hand, I sip slowly as I watch Paige sleep. In my bed. I feel like I need to pinch myself because I must be dreaming.

As I contemplate how the hell I'm gonna get her back to her dorm without raising any eyebrows, she begins to stir. The soft moan she expels makes my dick twitch in my pajama bottoms.

I blow on the curls of steam from my mug as I watch, amused, as she opens her eyes and blinks them rapidly. Her beautiful baby blues find mine quickly, and her brow furrows. "Headmaster?"

I frown. I thought we got past that last night when I was buried balls-deep inside her tight heat. I force a smile. "I'm pretty sure you can call me Anton now."

She sits up, yawns, and stretches. "Coffee? Anton?" she asks as she rakes her sleepy, lusty gaze across my bare chest.

I nod and pick up the mug I'd poured for her. Two creams, one sugar. I watched her prepare coffee so many times on the cafeteria camera that I have it memorized.

I'm such an obsessed fucking stalker…

I set it on the nightstand, and then sit on the bed next to her. "Good morning, baby girl."

"I can't believe you have this big-ass house out here. It's so nice, too." She picks up the coffee and blows on it as she looks around my massive master suite.

Chuckling, I reply, "It's not big."

Her gaze lazily drifts down to my lap. Admittedly, I've got a three-quarter leaner in my pants that is promising to become one-hundred percent hard in a few seconds. Just seeing her in my bed, naked and sated, arouses me. After bringing her back here last night, we'd made love two more times and I'm now officially all-consumed with her.

"It is, though." Her gaze slowly lifts from my crotch to my face. She grins. "Thank you for the five orgasms last night."

I lean down and press my lips to hers. "I can't say it was hard work or a sacrifice. But you're welcome."

We kiss gently, my tongue softly stroking her beautiful lips, my dick now fully standing at attention.

She pulls back and smiles at me. Then, she sips the coffee and sighs in contentment. "Perfect."

Ignoring my needy cock, I reply, "Two creams, one sugar. Just how you like it."

Her brow furrows. "How do you know…"

I throw her a grin. "I know everything."

"Never mind. Where's my phone? Astrid will be wondering why I didn't come 'home' last night." She uses her fingers to make air quotes.

"It's probably on the floor next to your clothes." I point. "But you don't have to worry because Astrid spent the night in Axel Tanaka's room last night."

She pauses her sipping. "How the hell do you know that?"

I lean down, kiss her on the head, and say, "I have my ways."

Paige scowls up at me, but I just laugh. "If you're a good girl, I'll tell you later." I curl some hair behind her ear. "Now get up. Let's have breakfast."

She perks at the mention of food and I stand up from the bed and help her up. My gaze drifts salaciously over her bare-naked body and I can't believe how lucky I am. Full tits, curvy hips, flat stomach, round ass, and a nearly bare pussy any man would worship.

"Like what you see?" she asks as she reaches for her pink panties.

I chuckle. "Oh, yeah." I reluctantly leave the room with a painful boner behind my pajama bottoms and go into the kitchen. As I'm dishing up the eggs and pancakes I made, she comes in wearing my button-up dress shirt the pink panties.

Holy fuck, that's sexy as shit. I swallow hard. "Sit," I command, pointing to the dining room table.

She nods and obeys.

I set the plate in front of her, then bring mine to the table as I sit.

"By the way, where did you get the dye for your underwear?" I nod my head at her lap.

She chokes on the bite of pancake and picks up her orange juice. After a big swig, she laughs. "It's not dye. Well, not really."

I raise an eyebrow, my eggs paused at my mouth in waiting.

She lifts a shoulder and says, "Kool-Aid leaves a pretty permanent stain. Not even those high-powered washers in the laundry rooms in the dorms gets it out."

I sit stunned for a few seconds, and then I just laugh. "Clever."

"And kind of smelly," she replies before shoveling a bite into her mouth.

Furrowing my brow, I ask, "Smelly… how?"

She hesitates before answering, "Breckon asked why my pussy smelled like watermelon."

The visual of the vampire's lips, tongue, face, or cock anywhere near Paige's beautiful cunt makes my pulse race and my blood heat up. I know I need to get used to the idea that I'll be sharing her, but it's going to be hard. My jaw tics in annoyance, and I'm rewarded with a triumphant grin on her face.

"He can eat pussy pretty damn good—for a kid." She forks eggs into her mouth and stares me down, as if gauging my reaction.

I can't act jealous. It'll piss her off and I'll lose her, I just know it. I lift my chin and reply, "I promise you I can last much longer than he can. My tongue and lips will have you screaming my name at least three times before I fuck you."

Her eyes widen and she stops chewing.

I grin and take a swig of coffee.

"You should have shown me those skills last night."

"I was too busy giving you orgasms with my fingers and cock," I reply, reaching down to grip my poor engorged dick. I just can't believe we're having this conversation. At my breakfast table.

"True," she says, chuckling.

We continue to eat in a comfortable silence, and when I can see she's done, I get up and put our plates into the sink. After that, I offer her my hand and drag her back into my master suite. There, I remove my shirt from her body and then her Kool-Aid pink panties, gazing at her body once again. "So damn gorgeous," I whisper before kissing her.

Her body instinctively leans in to mine and I walk us toward the bathroom. I only break the kiss to turn on the shower. The glass-encased granite shower with three showerheads blares to life as I flip the handle to turn it on. I continue to make love to her mouth with my tongue and lips while it heats up.

After shimmying out of my pajama bottoms, I walk us under the water. She groans in pleasure as the pulsating showerhead assaults her back and neck. Without warning, she jumps into my arms and wraps her legs around my waist, all while never breaking our kiss. I press her up against the wall and lean down to pull a pert pink nipple into my mouth. She groans and arches her head back against the wall. We're both soaking wet from the water, and I lift my head from her breast and look into her face. After setting her down on her feet, I kneel on the shower floor and lick my lips. I slowly spread her folds with my fingers and moan at the sight of her raw sex in my face.

She looks down at me, eyes wide, and then cries out when my tongue begins its slow and sensual assault on her engorged clit. Her legs widen as she puts one foot on the built-in shower stool. I continue to give attention to her delicious bundle of nerves as I slip two fingers inside her tight channel and pump them in and out, grinning as she begins to shake and quietly whimper. After giving her tender bud a few more hard sucks and licks, she breaks apart, a quivering mass of femininity and hormones while screaming out her release with my name and God's spilling from her lips.

I have to catch her before she slumps to the floor, which is easy because she's so small. I lean up and kiss her under the assault from the hot water. "I love you, Paige," I breathe.

Her slitted eyes widen and then she smiles. "I love you, too, Anton."

I want to yell and punch my fist in the air, but instead, I say, "Good, because I'm gonna fuck you hard now, baby girl."

She nods for a split second before I turn her around, press her upper body down toward the shower stool, and grip her hips. I line up my cock with her soaking wet and swollen sex and plunge inside. She's so damn tight, wet, and pulsating, I don't know how long I'm gonna last.

Paige groans her approval, her hands pressed flat on the shower stool as I assault her pussy, my cock plunging in and out at a punishing pace, seeking my release. I almost come when I hear her whimper and her walls tighten around my shaft. With one hand on her hip, I use the other to reach around and slide a finger over her sensitive clit. She bucks against me and cries out. Her cunt tightens around me even more and I can barely breathe with how hard she's working her hips, deliberately trying to milk me.

Her hips and ass slam back against my pelvis as she cries out, "Oh, Anton!" I just can't last any longer after watching that. A shiver races down my spine as my entire pelvis explodes. I still my thrusts and grip her hips tightly as my hot cum shoots deep inside her. And as we move in sync, finishing our releases, I just can't help but wonder how the fuck I'm ever gonna share this perfect, beautiful woman with anyone else.

Chapter 21

Paige

I hate lying. I really, *really* do. But the look on Astrid's face demands answers.

After I left Anton's place, I walked back toward the main Academy grounds, contemplating my dilemma. He insisted on giving me a ride on the golf cart he uses to move around campus and to his home and back, but I refused. I needed some time to think—to separate my hormones and emotions from reality.

I know it's no coincidence that I read about the Coresh Accord in Gram's spellbook and then Anton mentioned it as we were down in his dungeon… basement… lair… whatever it is. There's something bigger going on, and I'm dying to talk to my bestie about it, but I swore to Anton that I wouldn't tell anyone about our relationship. It has to remain a secret, even to her. Which kills me inside.

"How do you know I didn't come home last night?" I ask her in deflection as I turn on the water and wet my toothbrush.

"Because I was here, and you weren't."

"I was taking a walk, thinking about things." I cringe internally at the lame half-lie.

She narrows her eyes. "No, you were with one of the boys, weren't you?"

I tilt my head and plaster on a smile. "You got me. I was with one of the guys." Technically, not a lie. Thinking back to Griggs's comment, and knowing she can't know what I know, I say, "Well, you usually spend Friday nights with Axel is all I'm saying. I didn't think you'd miss me."

She sighs and plops down on her bed. "I did, but we got into a fight so I came back here about three a.m."

I spit toothpaste in the sink and then rinse my mouth out with water. After wiping my mouth on a towel, I head over to her bed and sit down. "Why are you fighting?"

She lifts a shoulder and looks down at the ground. "I don't even know anymore."

I place my hand on her arm. "Is it about sex?"

She nods slightly. "Yeah. Mostly."

"He's still not giving it up?" I ask.

"Pretty much." She looks up at me, her bottom lip quivering. "Why doesn't he want me?"

My heart breaks at her expression and I hug her. "Maybe he's just super shy?"

She laughs bitterly. "No, he's not shy. We've messed around. I've seen him naked. He's seen me naked. I've touched him. He's touched me. He just won't… seal the deal."

"Perhaps he's afraid he'll get you pregnant?" I'm grasping at straws here, I know, but I suck at comforting.

"He knows he can't. I'm a witch and he's a djinn. It's impossible." She sniffs.

Something Axel said occurs to me. "But he said his mom's a witch and his dad's a djinn. Maybe that's why?"

She pulls back and stares at me. "Oh, yeah. That's right. Then why doesn't he just say so?"

I shrug. "Maybe it's the shyness thing again. Pregnancy is a weird thing to bring up in a new relationship."

Astrid nods in agreement,

"Look, in the meantime, I'll snag a condom from Jory or Breckon and bring it to you. If he still won't have sex with you after being given one, we'll know there's something else going on."

Astrid sniffs and nods. "Thanks, girl. I know I shouldn't be so upset over this stupid stuff. I'm probably PMSing."

"It's not stupid," I quickly say. "It's in our nature to feel wanted. You have every right to be upset."

"What would I do without you?" she asks, smiling at me behind sad eyes.

"You'd be *sooo* bored and lonely." I stick out my tongue.

"That's true." She chuckles.

"C'mon," I say, standing up. "Let's go get dinner and then take a walk."

After dinner, we walk around the massive track set out just past the Olympic-sized pool. It seems like it's for a track for team competition, but I've yet to see us compete against anyone but each other. I've come out here alone a few times to think, and decided Astrid needed some fresh air and thinking time. I'll admit I'm in need of it myself.

My head is abuzz with confusion and conflict. Last night I spent with Anton was damn near magical. Honestly, a real treat—sleeping in a soft, comfortable bed, multiple orgasms, home-cooked food, and a few hours of Netflix and chill as we binge-watched some series about serial killers most of the day before I made the lone trek back to the dorms. It was so mundane, yet, almost like a luxury after being locked up here for the past six months.

Nights with Jory and Breckon are nice too, but not the same, obviously.

I want so badly to spill everything to my bestie. The night with Anton, the origins behind Fembot, the fact that, yes, the Coresh Accord is very real and that it's going to involve me.

Instead, I just let her vent about how she missed her family, and her frustrations with Axel. Letting her talk help melt away my stress about my current predicament involving three sexy-ass men who want me, and it helps me focus on her problems instead of my own.

I told her about my suspicions about me being part of the Coresh Accord spell that night and she blew me off. Saying it was an old wives' tale and it didn't really happen. She even said that immortality was impossible and definitely a pipe dream. I dropped the subject that night, just to find myself in Griggs's arms later, him fucking me hard and deliciously up against the wall of his secret lair.

My sex involuntarily clenches at the memory. The thought of how he could get me pregnant still lingers in the back of my mind and I hope the birth control pills I swiped from my purse would be effective.

I shake off those thoughts as I try hard to concentrate on Astrid and her problems.

"I don't even think my mom is gonna let me come live with her once I get outta here," she says as we continue our power-walk.

"Why not?" I ask, confused. I thought she and her mom had a good relationship.

"She's, like, pissed at me. For embarrassing her and the family by getting sent here."

I snort and wave a hand. "She doesn't have a very good imagination, then. My mom told all her friends I was at an exclusive academy in the mountains getting a pristine college education."

Astrid laughs. "Yeah, well, you're getting an education, all right. Not sure if it's pristine or not, but you'll come out a sex goddess."

We both laugh.

"You will, too, girlfriend. Don't worry. He'll come around."

She reaches over and squeezes my hand. "I hope you're right."

I flick a hand at her. "I'm always right."

We laugh again. I'm glad we have this time together to melt our stress away and get some much-needed exercise.

The way Jory's eyeing me in Occult Studies class makes me nervous. Normally, he just looks lusty or starry-eyed, but today is different. I try to ignore him and Breckon to soak up some learning—we have midterms coming—but I just can't. He's acting weird and I know after class I'll be getting cornered. This isn't my first motherfuckin' rodeo.

I exit class, flanked by Astrid, and don't bother trying to fast-walk to get away from them. I'm currently fixated on Anton and our secret relationship. It's been a week since our overnight rendezvous but he's constantly on my mind. Additionally, so are the vampire and dragon. It's so confusing to me. Confusing, yet exciting. Nothing like a self-esteem boost to have three men wanting you.

I stop to take a sip from the water fountain outside the classroom. When I stand up, Jory and Breck are there.

"Come to swim practice tonight. We need to talk to you," Jory says, Breckon at his side nodding his agreement.

Breckon glances at Astrid, who has her back turned and is chatting with Rainlily, then pierces me with this black stare. "Alone."

I nod. "I can do that. What's this about?"

Jory's jaw clenches and his gaze roves around the hallway

before he replies, "Pretty much the same thing we talked about in the library, only we have additional things to discuss. It's fu…flipping important, so make sure you're there."

Jory then pushes me up against the wall next to the fountain and cages me in with his arms. He leans down and whispers, "If you don't show up, we'll fucking hunt you down and make you pay for it."

A delicious shiver runs down my spine and my nipples pebble in response to his closeness. I suck in a breath and nod. Then I glance at Breckon, who's smiling salaciously at me. "He's not kidding," the vampire reiterates.

"I got it, I got it," I say, gently pushing Jory away from me. Students have stopped in the hallway to watch the interaction, and that's attention I don't need. It's bad enough that I'm gossiped about daily. Not that I don't deserve it. I mean, I really am fucking three different dudes. I'd gossip about me, too.

Astrid grabs my arm. "Let's go, we have two minutes to get to Magic."

I chance a glance back at the boys, who are walking toward the gym for their next class. Breckon flicks his gaze over his shoulder at me and gives me a panty-melting smile. I turn back around and wonder, for the hundredth time, just what the hell I've gotten myself into. Three dudes… and they all want me? How is that even possible?

We arrive at the Practical Magic building and my sexy headmaster is already instructing students to sit in a circle. We obey, and before he starts his lecture, Caleb worms his way in between me and Jack, who isn't even paying attention.

"Hi," Caleb says.

I bump him with my elbow. "Hi, yourself."

He glances at Griggs, who's standing there flipping through a large book in his hands, then back at me. "I have good news."

My heartrate increases. "Oh, my God. Give it to me."

"I had a dream about your grand-mama."

My eyes go wide. "You did? Tell me everything!"

"Later," he says, glancing at the headmaster. "I promise. I just want you to know that I have news for you."

"You frickin' tease!" I say, punching his arm good-naturedly.

"Tease is my middle name, girlfriend," he says, flashing me a megawatt smile with his perfect-as-hell straight, white teeth.

"Class, please stand and hold hands. *Do not* break the circle," Griggs says.

We all do as he says. I've got Caleb's hand holding my left and Astrid's on my right.

"Repeat after me," Griggs commands. "Mother of light, father of dark, combine your power, show us your mark."

We repeat the chant, and I wonder what the hell is going on.

"Mother of light, father of dark, combine your power, show us your mark," Griggs repeats.

We parrot him once again, and the last word is barely out of our mouths when the entire class screams and falls to the mats below us.

A searing, burning pain infuses itself on my right shoulder blade and I hiss out a curse under my breath. I sit up and try to regulate my breathing so I don't have a damn stroke.

Caleb looks at me wide-eyed.

Astrid's eyes are moist with unshed tears and terror.

I glance at Griggs, who is staring at me curiously.

With my left hand, I reach around and place it gently over my shoulder to touch my upper back. The area is sensitive to the touch and still burns like the fires of hell.

With careless abandon, I strip off my red sweater and button-up white shirt. Standing there in my light-purple sports bra, I pull the strap down and turn my back to Astrid. "What the he…ck is it?"

Rubbing her own back, she peers at me. The rest of the class closes in. "It's… it's…"

"It looks like a tattoo," Jack McAllister comments.

"What's it of?" I ask.

Astrid fishes her phone from her pocket and snaps a photo. She pushes the phone into my face.

I glance once at Griggs, whose arms are folded across his chest, an amused look on his face, then to Astrid's phone. An angry red symbol is carved into the top of my shoulder blade and it looks an awful lot like an infinity symbol.

"An eight?" Alicia whispers, her face peering close to it.

"It's an infinity symbol," Astrid comments.

The students begin stripping off their shirts. Griggs does nothing to stop them.

Each student has a different symbol carved into their backs. I don't know what any of them mean, but it's somewhat amusing watching everyone take photos of it to show the person, then the other person reciprocating.

But… the most amusing part is watching Griggs's face. He must get off on this part of the training. As I stare into his infuriatingly handsome face, I rack my brain to try to remember if I ever saw any kind of odd symbol "tattooed" on my mother or grandmother. I can't recall a thing—but then again, I'd really never seen either of them naked. In swimsuits, yes, but mostly lying on lounge chairs in the backyard, sunning themselves, reading books, their backs not visible.

What the hell does this mean?

I think back to the spell as Anton and I continue our stare-off. His gaze is boring so deep into mine that I feel like I'm going to combust from the inside. It's as if he's telling me to reach deep down into myself to find the reason for the symbol.

An infinity symbol? Why was I marked with it?

It'll grant the four of us immortality. We'll be able to be together forever. I remember Griggs's promise.

I gasp. That's why I've received this mark. It's my…

"…Destiny," Griggs comments to the class. "Now put your shirts back on."

I look up to see him directing the class to reclothe themselves.

I glance at Astrid's mark and hers is a circle with arrows through it, a heart in the middle. I snap a picture for her and hand her my phone.

Her eyes stare widely at it. "That's a kindness symbol." She looks up at me, almost frightened. "Do I need to be more kind to people?"

I take my phone back and thrust it into my sweater pocket since I've re-dressed. "No, girl. I think it means you're destined for a life of being kind to others. Just as you've done for me."

She smiles and visibly relaxes.

I look at Caleb's bare back. A triangle with an eye drawn in the center decorates his upper back. He glances at me over his shoulder. "Don't bother describing it. I had a dream about it last night. Triangle, creepy eye. Illuminati sh… stuff?"

I nod.

"That's what I thought. It's the sigil of psychics. I was gonna get a tat of it anyway. Griggs's spell saved me some cash." He chuckles and shoves his T-shirt over his head, followed by his white button-up shirt.

Staring at Caleb, I can't wait to hear what he has to say about my gram.

Chapter 22

Biting my lip, I stare up at Breckon. He brushes the towel over his spiky black hair and then rubs it over his face, all while not breaking eye contact with me. The water droplets on his face are sexy, and I have to resist the urge to lick them off his full lips.

"Thank you for coming," Jory whispers as he sits next to me on the bleachers. He wears just his swim speedo and a towel around his waist. His red hair is damp, and he still has the ring from his goggles around his eyes.

I feel like I'm the filling of a sex Oreo as I sit here between them. The heat they both generate makes me want to strip my clothes off and go dive into the massive Olympic-sized pool to cool the hell off.

"We know Griggs talked to you about the Coresh Accord," Breckon starts, his finger trailing up my bare arm.

I look up at him and smile into his handsome face. "He did."

"How do you feel about that?" he asks, and judging by the burning lust in his gaze, I have to resist the urge to look down at what is probably a straining erection against his towel.

"Honestly, I don't know. Do we really wanna live forever? I mean, that sounds boring and kind of expensive."

Jory barks out a laugh, and it's then I notice he's got his thick, pale hand on my thigh. I look down at it, then up at him. "What's so freakin' funny, dragon breath?"

"Never grow old. Never die. Never deal with the complaints or aches and pains of our parents and grandparents? Sounds like a dream." Breckon's mouth is dangerously close to my ear.

I fear if I turn my head, he'll kiss me… and as much as I

want that, I also know I'll end up on camera getting fucked ten ways 'til Sunday if I do. So I keep my gaze locked on the still-rippling pool. "I don't know. It's a hard decision."

"It's not, though."

I look at Jory, whose comment is still washing over me. "You guys prepared to move here permanently? Because from what Griggs told me, he's stuck-like-Chuck here. He's the headmaster for the next twenty-odd years and can't leave. Family obligations and all that."

Jory lifts a shoulder and lets it fall. "Who cares? Twenty years is nothing compared to eternity. I can kick it here. Maybe we can even get jobs as teachers and coaches and sh... stuff."

Breckon chimes in, "Yeah, then we'll be free to come and go as we please."

I'm about to retort about how boring Montana is when Breck begins to lick my neck and then up to my face. Jory does the same, and the dual sensation makes me shudder violently. I feel Jory's thick hand move up my thigh and the thought that Griggs is probably watching it on his computer turns me on even more.

I crane my neck back to give each guy better access. I stare into the clear March star-shot sky and can't believe I'm in this predicament. All three of them want to complete the Coresh Accord, and I seem to be the starring headliner in it... but why me? They told me it's imperative that all three of them love me. So is it true? They are all in love with me?

Anton told me that he is. So why haven't these two?

My mind swirls with so many things. How does this work? The three of us live together in some kind of polyamorous arrangement? Do the guys fall in love with each other, too? Do they have sex with each other, or just me?

That would be pretty hot to watch...

Confusion and overthinking begin to choke me, so I stand up to give myself a minute to breathe.

"What's wrong, baby?" Breckon asks, grabbing my hand.

I snatch it away and tromp down the bleachers to the sidewalk below. The beams of the almost full moon rain down on me and I stand there, trying to catch my breath. With my hands on my knees, I bend forward to steady my breathing.

Once I feel more balanced, I gaze up at the two handsome supes and say, "I can't do this. I love you both. I love Anton. But it's too much. I can't breathe. I'm suffocating!"

With that, I turn on my heel and run away from the pool area. I keep running until I find myself in the field that stretches between the Academy and the faculty's housing area. Griggs's house is yards away, and as tempting as it is to knock on his door and let me sleep away my stress, wrapped in his heat and security, I know I need to resist. I need to be alone and find a way to ground myself.

Remembering the Stile in my room, I sprint back to my dorm room, relieved when I find it empty. I love Astrid, but I can't deal with her or anyone right now. I pull the Stile out of her nightstand drawer and draw upon my memories of Magic 101 instruction. I cannot recall the rune I'm searching my memory bank for, so I go to my messenger bag, flip it open, and find my notes. Furiously flicking through them, I smile when I find what I'm looking for.

Without hesitation, I draw the calming rune onto my arm and take some yoga breaths. I kick off my shoes, and within mere minutes, I'm lying on my bed, the power of sleep encompassing me within its depths.

"Paige…"

I turn around to see Caleb swagger toward me. I'm standing outside the male dorms, pacing, as the night has turned chilly and I'm trying to keep warm. I don't even know what I'm doing out here except that my anxiety has me stressed to the max and I'm trying to figure out what the fuck I'm gonna do about this whole Coresh Accord bullshit. I slept a couple hours but then I was wide awake at two a.m.

"Let's sit," he says, dragging me by the hand to the nearest bench.

I sit down next to him, happy to soak up his warmth and charisma. "Whatcha got for me?"

"Damn, girl. You just gonna hit the gas like that?" he asks, amusement twinkling in his light-brown eyes.

I laugh. "Sorry. It's just that it's cold and I've been dying all day to find out about my gram.

He rubs my arm, his fingers igniting a flame. "I know."

I lean my head on his shoulder and sigh. "Tell me everything."

I can feel his chest rise and fall. "First and foremost, your grand-mama wasn't killed by no vampire."

Lifting my head from his shoulder, I stare wide-eyed into his face. "What?"

"My dreams are never wrong, or inaccurate, Paige," he states matter-of-factly.

"I'm not questioning them… or you… I'm… I'm… just in a bit of shock, that's all."

"Understandable," he replies. "It's just that… my dreams are pretty accurate but sometimes open to interpretation."

"You're freakin' killing me here," I murmur from my place on his shoulder.

"Paige… your grandma was killed by your"—he clears his throat—"your father."

I gasp so hard I may pass out. Lifting my head up to stare

into his eyes, I say, "No. No, that can't be right. You're wrong." I shake my head. "That can't be true. My mom would have said something if she knew who her killer was."

He shakes his head. "I'm not wrong, Paige. I'm sorry."

I sigh, not knowing what to say to that. The only thing I know is that me and my mom are going to be having a serious conversation about this tomorrow.

I try to formulate words, but nothing comes. I numbly stare off into nothing.

Caleb squeezes my hand. "Are you okay? Should I have not told you that?"

I shake my head. "No. I mean, yes. I'm glad you told me, but it's a lot to unpack—a lot to believe. I just don't know…"

"I'm sorry," Caleb whispers, planting a kiss on the top of my head.

"Don't be," I reply. I'm suddenly feeling tired, weary, downright exhausted. "I have so many problems right now that I don't know how to deal with them all. I'm drowning, Caleb."

"I know, spicy witch," he replies, hauling me closer to his heat. "Just vent to me. You have my full attention."

"Between this, and the three guys wanting me all at once, sometimes it's just… it's too fucking much," I whisper.

"Definitely." He looks down at me and smooths my hair back. "Just know that any girl—or guy—would absolutely fucking kill to be in your shoes."

I nod and laugh sardonically. "I doubt that."

Caleb pulls me off his shoulder and grips both of mine. "Think about it, Paige. You're destined for something bigger—greater. Until you grasp that, you'll continue to be a mass of twisted emotions with no real goal ahead."

"I'm just fucked up," I admit, suddenly choking on a sob as Caleb grabs my hand and demands my attention.

He shakes his head. "No, you're not. You're caught between a rock and hard place, as my grandad says."

Thinking about the silly metaphor, I decide he's right. "What the heck am I gonna do, though?" I slide my hand over my head to smooth the stray hairs that escaped my ponytail back down.

"You can't escape your destiny, girlfriend." He mock jaw-punches me.

"But why? Why is it my destiny to be the witch in this Coresh Accord bullsh... nonsense?"

Caleb flashes me a smile. "I don't know, honey. It just happens that way. No way to stop it. And sheesh... why you complaining, anyway? You got three smokin' hot dudes chasin' your tail. Get it, girl!"

He's right... I need to stop bitching and whining about my predicament. I file his bombshell revelation about my gram and dad into the back of my mind. I can't deal with that right now. I need to focus on getting the hell out of here.

Not once did I ever think coming to this "prison" academy was going to end up like this.

Not once did I ever stop to contemplate what this Academy would do for my life... my future.

And not one fucking time did I think that I would fall in love with three beautiful men who all wanted me all to themselves, but also knew they had to share.

What have I done to deserve this curse... this fate... this destiny?

LARCHWOOD CORRECTIVE ACADEMY SERIES

Curses & Charm

Monsters & Magic

Runes & Rituals

Secrets & Spells

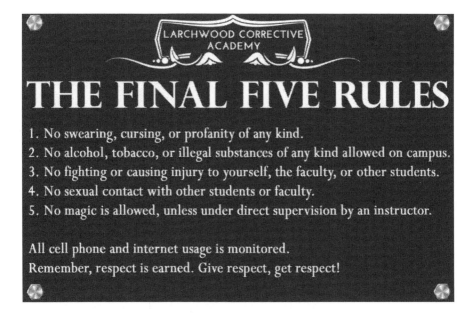

ABOUT THE AUTHOR

C.J. is a USA Today bestselling author living in Colorado but wishes she was someplace warmer. She loves the SF 49ers and has a weakness for expensive shoes. She's the author of over 40 novels and short stories that contain both fantasy and paranormal romance with kickass heroines and strong alphas. Having recently retired from a twenty-year career in federal law enforcement, she's looking forward to the next chapter in life.

She can be found on Facebook, Instagram, and on her website, cjpinard.com.

Use your device's QR code reader to get a link to all of C.J.'s books!

Made in the USA
Middletown, DE
07 October 2022